HIDE AND SEEK

Jill Collins

Publishing History

May 2017

Published by JC AXIOM

This book is based on fiction. Characters, names, occurrences, places and incidents are not real and are the product of the author's imagination or are used fictitiously. Any resemblance to actual persons, living or dead, events, or locales is entirely coincidental.

Cover design by BA Advertising Graphics-Bernadette August

Author photograph copyright © by Jill Collins

THE HOLY BIBLE, NEW INTERNATIONAL VERSION ®, NIV® Copyright © 1973, 1978, 1984, 2011 by Biblica, Inc. TM Used by permission. All rights reserved worldwide.

ISBN 978-0-9964515-5-0

Manufactured in the United States of America

DEDICATION

God.

ACKNOWLEDGMENTS

To my family members and my friends that are like family, thank you so much for the prayers. I couldn't have done this without you or Him. To the usual crew: Kim for your spirit; Lydia for your ear; Eric for your encouragement; Christian for your smile; Gladys and Katheryn for your eyes. Finally, to the courageous many that have gotten help for drinking, depression, smoking, overeating, anger, narcotics, gambling, debting, under-earning, hoarding, any mental or emotional illness, thank you for slowly tearing down the walls of shame.

❧ CHAPTER 1 ❧

The grand floor-to-ceiling-windowed room was packed. Loud, pulsating music thumped through the air, in competition with the voices of a rather large group of well-dressed partygoers. I was in Algiers Point on the west bank of New Orleans, at the home of bestselling author and motivational speaker Donovan Quinn for the launch party of his latest book, *Fix Your Life.*

"Did you hear that?" I suddenly yelled over the noise to my date, Assistant D.A. Jay Childs.

"What?" he responded.

"Sounded like a gunshot!"

"What? No, I didn't hear anything Morgan, other than that song calling us out onto the dance floor," the raw-boned, boyishly handsome man told me, as he reached for my hand.

I downed the last bit of wine from my glass and placed it on a tray. He pulled me in close to his rock-hard frame, and we began to move in harmony to the music. A piece of his perfectly coifed cold, black hair fell onto his tanned forehead as he chanted the name of the song: "Ohhhh, It Ain't My Fault."

Jay and I and the other partygoers soon began to form a line, strutting and dancing behind the brass band of musicians. We were having fun. I soon distanced my mind from the loud noise I thought I had heard.

"Excuse me," I told my date in his ear after we had danced to more than a few songs, "I'll be back." I looked into his deep, dark eyes and abruptly left his side. His furrowed brow displayed compliant surprise at my interruption of the good time we were having. Nonetheless, I was gone from his presence in a flash. I had spotted Commander Jackson Slade standing on the other side of the room. "Pardon me, pardon me," I offered up as I slithered through the crowded area.

"Hey, everybody!" the basketball-like tall, dark-haired, guest of honor yelled out to the horde in that melodic New Orleans accent. "Hey, everybody!" he bellowed again before he slashed his long, pale-complexioned hand across his neck, signaling the musicians to stop playing. The house lights came on, and the crowd began to simmer down. Everyone's attention was drawn toward the stage. A dim light glimmered over Dr. Quinn's strikingly white teeth as he began to speak.

"Before this night comes to an end," he began, "I just wanna thank y'all so much for coming out. Can't tell you what it means to have so many that mean so much to me here tonight celebrating the release of my latest book, *Fix Your Life*."

The bass drum pounded as the partygoers cheered.

"Where is she?" Dr. Quinn continued. "I know she's here. I want to start by thanking someone that has been so instrumental in helping me define key parameters for *Fix Your Life.* She answered every question, and took every call. Y'all know her as the psychiatric crime-solving sleuth extraordinaire. But I know her as a great literary colleague, and I'm now proud to call her a friend, She's a credit to her profession and a credit to the city of New Orleans—and she's not bad to look at, either. Folks, Dr. Morgan Winters, show yourself. Where are you?"

"He's talkin' 'bout you, Dr. Winters," a partygoer informed me.

"There she is!" Dr. Quinn called out. "Wave to the folks, Morgan. To Dr. Morgan Winters. Isn't she gorgeous?"

The toast caught me off-guard. I made awkward eye contact with a few of the smiling faces standing nearby and waved to the guest of honor.

"Can I take a picture with you, Dr. Winters?" asked another partygoer. "I've read about all your cases, and I have both of your books. I just love you. Can I take a picture?"

"Oh—ahh, sure," I responded, smiling for the camera and posing for the selfie with the lady.

"Thank you so much, Doctor."

"You're welcome."

Once that was over, I continued on my way through the crowd. "Excuse me," I told a strikingly attractive, pale-complexioned woman impeding my progress. She seemed oblivious to the sound of my voice as she stood in my way, for her eyes were fixated on the guest of honor. "Excuse me," I told her again, this time with a little more volume, but still to no avail. *Humph,* I thought. *Whatever!* was my next thought as I found my way around the lady in red and continued to quasi-listen to Dr. Quinn speak.

"I can hardly say thanks to anybody without saying thank you to Simon & Steele Publishing, and you, Redmann Steele, for the support you and your crew have given me. To the best damn publisher a writer could have, hear, hear! And to a man I now call 'friend.' " He languished onto the commandingly tall, freckle-faced Redmann Steele.

"If I might add just a few words?" Steele interrupted as he paced through the crowd and toward the stage. "As part owner of Simon & Steele Publishing,

I can tell you, Donovan Quinn is a rare gem. He does the grunt work that people just don't want to do anymore. And he's quite the bookseller. It's been a pleasure to know him, and I'm glad to be able to call him a friend. To Donovan Quinn, and *Fix Your Life*!"

I stopped to get a glimpse of the two men standing next to each other with raised glasses. Suddenly, though, someone's hand touched my right shoulder, quickening my mind and my vision away from Quinn and Steele.

"Where ya at, Wintahs?" the deep, raspy voice inquired as I turned around to see the chiseled jaw of my old friend.

"Slade!" I shot back. "How you doing?" We hadn't seen each other up-close and personal in a while. The NOPD—or, rather, Superintendent Bryson—called himself "spreading the wealth." So I had been working with other detectives, only seeing my old friend and first partner in solving crime, Commander of Specialized Investigations Jackson Slade, in passing.

"If I was doin' any better, Wintahs, One-A-Day would be takin' me. I'm good!" His crooked smile, against the backdrop of his deep-set brown eyes, quickly reminded me of how handsome he was.

"What are you doing here, Slade?"

"Friend of a friend invited me," he quickly added, and just as quickly went on. "Don't really know the guest of honor up there talkin'. Seems like a likable fella, though. I guess I don't have to ask what *you're* doin' here. I recognize your publisher over there. But I haven't seen *you* in a minute. So how ya doin'?"

His massive hand gently touched my sleeveless arm. Just as I was about to answer his question, though, an exotic, dark-haired young woman walked over and slid her hand into his. A strikingly beautiful golden pashmina was draped over one of her shoulders.

Oh, he's on a date, too, I thought. *I suppose she's the friend of a friend he didn't want to really talk about. Whatever, Morgan. Get over it. You haven't been around.*

I gut-checked myself and plastered on a fake smile.

"Wintahs, I'd like you to meet the friend of a friend I was tellin' you about, Lola Mendez," Slade said. "Lola's one of the guest of honor's research assistants. Lola, this is—"

"Oh, I *know* who this is, Jackie," the young beauty eagerly spoke. "How could I *not* know *thee* Dr. Morgan Winters, New Orleans' own psychiatric crime-solving sleuth? I've actually communicated with you before, on behalf of Dr. Quinn. Besides that, Jackie talks about you all the time. I'm..."

The good-looking woman went on talking as I began to multitask, feigning interest in what she was saying while attempting to read her body language. I was trying my best to find something wrong with

Slade's new girlfriend. *Steady, direct eye contact, shoulders back...feet evenly planted, no tapping or fidgeting...I guess she's okay*, I disappointedly thought as Ms. Mendez continued her palaver. But then she crossed her arms, and her tone, though it remained soft, grew sharp and more deliberate. *Hmmm, what's that? Maybe a little too confident? No, she's being competitive. With me? Oh, just stop, Morgan. You're biased.* I shut down my flawed assessment.

"...So, the countless hours I've been able to work with Dr. Quinn and be under his tutelage have proven to be invaluable. The things that he's taught me about life and the concepts of taking advantage of what it has to offer are immeasurable. It's given me life experiences that I'll never ever forget. Because of Dr. Quinn, I was able to finish at the top of my class—like you, Dr. Winters." The young woman proudly smiled.

"Well it certainly is a pleasure to meet you, Lola. And I wish you continued success."

Truth be told, it was anything but a pleasure, meeting Slade's date—but I truly did wish her well, professionally speaking. Then I thanked God in my head for small favors as we were suddenly interrupted by the guest of honor making another declamation.

"And finally, to my family, I'd like to start with my youngest two children, Donnie Jr. and Ashley. I know the two of you are at your friend's house right now, but, you know, Daddy loves you so much. You're the best part of me. Your innocent faces bring life to what I do."

The crowd released a collective sigh.

"And Aaron, my first-born son. Continue to work hard, son. That's what the Quinns do."

Donovan lifted his glass in the direction of his lanky, dark-haired son, who was standing in the back of the room.

"Hear, hear!" rang a voice from the crowd as glasses were raised and another toast was made.

"And last, but far from least, my beautifully perfect wife, Dane. Dane, I don't see you, but I know you're here. To you, my dear—wherever you are."

An affectionate sigh emanated from the packed room, followed by thunderous applause, as Quinn raised his glass high in the air.

"With that, I have one last thing that I want to say before we end the evening," he continued. "I want to thank you all once again for coming out, and *laissez les bons temps rouler!*"

Several men dressed in black tuxedos began to make their way through the crowd, passing out white umbrellas and handkerchiefs, formally paying homage to the second-line tradition of partying with an open parasol and waving a handkerchief. The brass band then set itself center-stage. The trumpet soulfully belted out the four musical notes signaling the second-line call for the last dance.

"There you are—this is for you!" Jay exclaimed as

he suddenly reappeared. He had commandeered one of the party-making parasols, which he handed to me. He flashed his pearly-whites, slid his hand into mine, and began to move to the lilt. I snuck a peak at Slade. He didn't see me. He was looking at Jay.

"Let's dance," I told my date.

*   *   *   *

"Morgan Winters, this is so good. I can't believe how packed it is in here at this time of night," Jay told me as he sucked on a crab leg he had scooped up from his now-empty bowl of gumbo at the Creole House restaurant, where the two of us were having a late night snack after the party. "I can't get enough of this stuff. Oh, excuse me."

He summoned the unrefined downhome waitress. "Can I have just a couple more pieces of French bread?" he asked her. "And could you have them toast it for me like you did before, you know, with extra butter?"

"Sure, dawlin'," responded the waitress. "Be back in a sec."

Jay wasn't from New Orleans. He was a mid-westerner—a beef-and-potatoes man. So the food down here was, as he put it, a taste of heaven every time. And that he could get a full meal at almost any hour of the day or night was icing on the cake.

"We should do this more often, Morgan." He wiped his mouth and flashed an innocent wide-eyed grin toward me. I enjoyed Jay's energy—his eager approach to life. He was a little younger than I preferred, but he was fun.

"Do what more often?" I asked.

"You know, go to a party; have a good time dancing; and then grab a full-course meal afterwards."

"Oh, *that* part."

"Yeah, this is the best. Been here for a year or so, but I can't get enough of this food."

"Been here all my life, Jay, and I'm still not over it."

"Here ya go, dawlin'," the waitress announced as she dropped off some more buttered French bread.

Jay shot out his hand to grab a piece, but then caught himself midway and politely offered the plate to me. "Care for another piece, Morgan?"

"No, I'm good. Have at it."

He went in two-fisted, seizing a slice with both hands. "And that party. That was something else. Can't get enough of that second line either. Who thought of that?"

"Well, Jay, if you really want to know..."

"Yeah, I want to know."

"The way they tell it, years ago—and I mean a *lot* of years ago—people would hang around after Mardi Gras parades or a jazz funeral procession."

"They didn't want the party to end, right?"

"You got it. They were generally trying to keep the party going."

"Maybe claim some kind of ownership to the event, too?"

"Maybe. Anyway, it eventually turned into an official thing—a second line."

"Why do they call it a 'second line'?"

"It's the second line after the parade line or the funeral procession line. Get it?"

"Oh, yeah, I love it," Jay responded with more than a trace of childlike excitement in his voice. Suddenly his gaze shifted away from me toward the clock on the wall. "Oh, dang!" he suddenly exclaimed. "Look at the time! I have an early-morning meeting. May I?" He reached for the last piece of bread, awaiting my approval.

"All yours," I consented. "You have a meeting on Saturday?"

"Yeah, I'm sorry, Morgan. I was having so much fun that I forgot what time it was. Are you ready?" Jay reached for his wallet and placed twenty bucks on the table.

"Ready." I wiped my mouth one last time and stood up as he stood behind me to pull my chair out. "This was fun, Jay," I told him as we proceeded toward my car.

"You're telling me. I had a blast."

He opened my car door, and once again slid his hand into mine. This time, though, he raised it up to his lips and softly kissed it. "Good night, Morgan. Can't wait to do it again," he said as his touch lingered before releasing my hand.

My mind quickly flashed back through the evening, seeing the two of us dancing, Slade, and then back to Jay in the present. "Good night, Jay, and, yes, this was quite enjoyable."

✧ CHAPTER 2 ✧

"Not too bad, midnight," I said out loud as I glanced at the clock on my dashboard while driving across the Crescent City Connection, also known as the Mississippi River Bridge.

Interesting evening, I thought. *I had a good time with Jay. In fact, I like him. Really? You like him.* I challenged my mind. *Is it him that you like, or is it the package that he comes in? He is good-looking.* I flashed back to the sight of his even bronzed skin covering his soaring cheekbones. *Umph, umph, umph. He is good-looking, and I do like him. He's fun. In a young, carefree kind of way. What about seeing Slade, on a date?*

"You know the answer to that question, Morgan Jane Winters," I chided myself out loud as I flipped a CD into the player as a distraction from my mind's eye. I bopped and nodded to the music before I realized what I was listening to: "On Your Face" by Earth, Wind, and Fire.

"Really?" I rhetorically asked the audio system in my car as I heard the lyrics melodically depict the reality of feelings being penned all over someone's face. I couldn't resist sneaking a peek at my reflection in the rearview mirror. "Yep, there they are, and so much more," I said as my eyes took in a flash of my own buried uneasiness.

Suddenly, though, a pair of fast-approaching headlights hijacked my image from the mirror. "What the hell?" I frowned as I questioned the speeding car. I quickly drove onto the narrow shoulder to avoid the reckless driver, but it was too late. Red-hot fear and icy panic engulfed my body from head to toe as I squeezed the steering wheel and braced myself for the inevitable.

BOOM! slammed the car into mine.

*   *   *   *

You're okay. You're okay, I told myself as I shook my head to clear the cobwebs. I wanted to sit for a moment to be in shock, but somehow I knew I didn't have that luxury. *I have to get out of here,* I thought as I futilely pulled and pushed the door handle in an attempt to open it. It was jammed. Taking a deep breath, and then summoning a dose of adrenalin- fueled strength, I thrust my shoulder into the door, alas, loosening it ajar.

"Thank you, Jesus!" I exclaimed as I stepped out of the wrecked vehicle.

What is that? I abruptly thought, spotting a hint of a flame under the mangled hood of the car that smashed into mine. I whipped out my phone and pressed 9-1-1.

"9-1-1, what is the nature of your emergency?" inquired the shrill monotone female voice on the other end of the line.

"There's been an accident on the CCC," I told her as I paced through the smolder and toward the other car. "Two drivers, one person injured, going eastbound, in the far right lane, before the Tchoupitoulas Street exit. One airbag deployed. We're going to need an ambulance." I peered through the other vehicle's cracked windshield. "And, please, while you're at it, send the Fire Department, too. I see flames under the hood of the other car."

"Okay, Ma'am, we have medical and fire units on the way. Are both drivers still in their cars?"

"Uhh—no. I'm one of the drivers. I'm no longer in my car."

"Well then, Ma'am, you should probably step as far away from both vehicles as you can. Is the other person out of their car?"

"Uhh, no, she's still in the car."

"Ma'am..." the operator began as I ended the call.

"Are you okay?" I yelled at the woman through the window of her now-crushed black sports car. I could hardly see her face. "You have to get out of there! Your car's on fire!" I shouted with the intention of jolting her into consciousness, but all she did was moan and groan. I opened her car door with a couple of tugs. White airbag powder covered the woman's face and clothes. "We have to get you out of here!" I yelled, suddenly bringing her to cough and gasp for air. I hurriedly reached inside to unbuckle her seat belt, but my sense of urgency was briefly interrupted by the smell of alcohol and the familiarity of the driver. *This is the lady from the party!* I thought. *And she's been drinking—a lot!*

CRACK! POW! snapped the festering blaze under the hood of her car as it grew more and more agitated.

Wonder what the story is here, I thought as I began to pull the barely conscious woman out of the car. I put one of her arms around my neck and then lifted her to her feet. "Lean on me," I instructed her as I supported the brunt of her weight. We walked as far away from the cars as my diminished strength would allow, before we collapsed onto the concrete ground of the bridge.

BOOM! erupted the car engine in a blaze.

Soon I heard the thin echo of sirens crescendoing through the noise of the burning vehicle. *Now you can be in shock, Morgan,* I told myself as I closed my eyes and gave into my mind and body's desire for a respite...

ᕦ CHAPTER 3 ᕤ

"Ouch!" I whispered out loud as I sat up and annoyingly reached for my aching neck. I have a particular disdain for the physical discomfort that comes from whiplash, not to mention the inconvenient irritation of an impromptu hospital stay. It's times like this that I have to make a conscious effort not to resort to old habits—you know, getting angry and marinating over things that I really don't have any control over—"the poor me's," is what I call it.

So, instead, I took a deep breath, looked at the heart monitor, closed my eyes, and began to count my blessings—literally. Let's see... *I survived an accident on the CCC—that's one. An accident and explosion on the CCC—that's two. I got a chance to see my buddy Slade—that's three—with another woman.*

I flippantly added, "Blessings, Morgan, blessings!"

out loud, admonishing myself back to the task at hand. I took another deep breath. "What else? What else?" *What about the other driver? What about the fact that you were able to help her out of her car, before it blew... yeah, absolutely?* I pursed my lips with a slight smile of fulfillment.

"Wait a minute!" I said out loud as I sat up with a jolt, interrupting the moment. "What's this?" I was referring to the small brown bag at the foot of my bed, with a note attached: *"Stopped by earlier. You were sleeping. Thought you could use these. Signed, Me."*

I opened the bag to see a pair of sweats and sneakers. *Too much,* I thought as I reached into the bag and pulled out the oversized red sweats. *Wait a minute.* The red sweats triggered a flashback to the party and the accident. *That's the same lady from the party, staring so intensely at Donovan Quinn, and that's the lady that ran into me.*

RING-RING, went the abrupt, unpleasant tone of my hospital phone, breaking my thought. *Who could that be?* I wondered as I picked up the old-fashioned, caller ID-less receiver.

"Morgan Jane Winters," said the oh-so-familiar, soft-spoken, yet frighteningly commanding voice on the other end of the phone.

Uh-oh. A brief wave of guilt and fear simultaneously swept through my body. Very few people called me by my full name. And only one person could elicit a stimulus response combination of fear, guilt, and then comfort by reciting my name: Vivian Winters, my mother. I knew I would be in for a tongue-lashing for not calling her. I didn't want her to worry, and that's true. But the complete truth is, that it's hard for me to maintain the tough veneer of Dr. Morgan Winters when Mother is around. I wanted to bulldoze my way right through this thing, the accident, and get back to my life. Not so easy to do with Mother.

"What happened?" she said. "Are you all right? We're on our way back to the states, right now. Morgan Jane, are you listening?"

"Yes, I'm listening, Mother, and I'm fine. You don't have to shorten your trip for this." She and my father were on vacation in the Bahamas.

"What happened, Morgan?"

"Just a little fender-bender." I flashed back to the vision of my mangled car, knowing it was far more than a fender-bender. "How did you find out about the accident anyway? You're not even in the country." My airy hope was that she would simply accept my vague answer, tell me how she found out about the accident, and decide to enjoy the rest of their vacation in Florida. But deep down, I knew better. I wouldn't accept that answer. Why *would* I expect her to?

"Never mind how I found out. What happened? A fender-bender doesn't put you in the hospital," she admonished.

"I was rear-ended, Mother. But I'm fine. They're

probably going to release me today. I know if you could be here you would, but there's no need, nor is there a need to worry. You and Daddy enjoy the rest of your trip, and I'll call you later on this evening when I get home, okay?" I could hear her exasperation through the phone.

"I just worry about you, Morgan. Since you've been working with the NOPD, you have to admit, some strange things have happened to you."

"Point taken, but I'm fine. Now, please enjoy the rest of your trip. Tell Daddy I love him, and I'll see the two of you when y'all get back."

"Morgan Jane Winters, you be careful, and I love you."

"I love you, too, Mother, and I will." I hung up the receiver. Feeling relieved that they were staying put, I mindlessly picked up the remote control to the TV. "What the—?" My almond-shaped eyes widened with surprise at what I was seeing and hearing.

"That's right, Allison," reported the news anchor. "As you can see, forensic experts continue to scour through the fire-ravaged home of famed author and motivational speaker Donovan Quinn here on Belleville Street in the historic Algiers Point area of the West Bank. Fire Chief Fletcher Wade told us that three people tragically died last night, after flames swept through the home you see behind me."

The video panned the half-burned house. The

charring stopped at the bright red front door of the two-storied Victorian home. "Neighbors said that in the wee hours of the morning a loud explosion-like noise could be heard from the direction of the Quinn home. Mr. Grayling Jones, who lives across the street from the Quinn home, told us this."

"I was asleep, and a loud noise woke me up," Mr. Jones began. "Eventually I got up and looked out the window to see flames coming from that side of the house. After I called 911, I looked out my window again and noticed Dr. Quinn and his son standing outside. They seemed pretty frazzled, especially young Aaron. The fire engine pulled up right after I went over to see if there was anything I could do. But there wasn't. They didn't get there quick enough. Dr. Quinn tried to go back in there for his wife, but they wouldn't let him. So he had ta' stand out there like the rest of us 'til they brought her out. Then they brought the two kids out. I never saw anything like that before—just awful."

"Thank you, Mr. Jones. As you just heard, tonight at approximately five a.m., what is believed to be a gas explosion turned fire claimed the lives of at least three people tonight, here in Algiers Point. Allison, back to you."

"This is awful!" I shouted as my cellphone began to ring. I reached to silence it, but before I could press the red decline button, I saw that it was Jay. I lowered the TV volume and took the call.

"Hello?" I forged a pleasant tone.

"Good morning, Beautiful. How are you?" The velvety-smooth voice on the other end of the phone greeted me. "I've been sending good thoughts your way."

"Good thoughts received," I casually replied. I knew he had no idea that I was speaking to him from a hospital bed. Something in me didn't quite want him to know just yet.

"Jay, have you seen the news?" I digressed, still focused on what I had just seen on TV.

"Yeah, I'm looking at it right now. What a mess, huh? From what I understand, it was just a terrible gas fire."

"I can't believe we were just there, I added as a dainty, petite-framed nurse entered my room.

"Morning, Dr. Winters," she said kindly. "I'm gonna take your temperature and blood pressure now, okay, Sweetie?"

"Temperature and blood pressure?" Jay inquired from the other end. "Where are you?"

"One second, Jay." The nurse placed the thermometer in my mouth. "I'm in the hospital," I inaudibly spoke with my mouth full.

"You're *where?* I don't think I heard you right. It sounded like I just heard you say that you were in the hospital."

"You heard right." The instrument beeped as the nurse removed it from my mouth. "I was in a little fender-bender, and I *am* in the hospital, Jay. I guess it was a little more than a fender-bender, huh? But I'm fine, as you can hear. And I'm pretty sure they're releasing me today."

The nurse continued her assessment.

"I don't know what to say,"

"Nothing to say, Jay. I'm fine."

"What happened? When?"

"I was on the CCC on my way home from the restaurant, and someone rear-ended me."

"The CCC!"

"Yeah, the CCC, but I'm fine. I didn't go into the river. All is well."

"I guess. Well, do you need anything?"

Before I could answer his question, a rap on the door abducted my attention. "Hold on a minute, Jay." I turned to the door. "Come in!" I adjusted my hospital gown so that it no longer hung off my shoulder.

"What's going on in here?" went an easy voice as the door began to open.

"Jay, can I call you back?"

"Sure. Call me back, okay?" he warmly requested.

"I will. I will. Talk to you later."

"I said, what's going on in here?" The warm twinkle of the visitor's light-brown eyes was the first thing I saw as he slowly peeped into the room. The rest of his six-foot-two frame stepped in to reveal a bouquet of colorful daisies from behind his back. It was Slade.

The round-faced nurse looked at my guest, grinned as she finished taking my vitals, and left the room.

"Let's see, what we got here?" Slade continued as he laid a bouquet of flowers down on the stand next to my bed and proceeded to scrutinize the bruise on my forehead. He twisted his mouth to the side, squinted his eyes, and lightly touched my chin with his forefinger, leaving the faint aroma of old-school cologne, Aramis.

"Well, Dr. Wintahs, from what I can see..." he proceeded in his most proper voice, articulating every syllable. He then stepped back, folded his arms, and continued to look me over in feigned contemplative thought. I gave him the same look back. I twisted my mouth to the side as well, but with a slight grin, as I stifled my desire to laugh. I couldn't wait to hear what he was going to say.

I miss him, I thought.

"Well Dr. Wintahs, after careful examination, it appears that what you have is not uncommon."

"Oh, really, Jackie?" I facetiously asked, reveling in the not-so-long-awaited opportunity to make fun of his new 'girlfriend's' pet name.

"Yes, really. And that's Dr. Jackie to you," Slade sarcastically replied, tilting his head forward and raising his left eyebrow. "Dr. Wintahs, you appear to have a boo-boo on your forehead."

I could no longer suppress my amusement. I released a hearty laugh as he stood there in pride-filled accomplishment, flashing his crooked smile and nodding his head. "Well, Doctor, what do you recommend?" I jokingly asked him, wiping the tears of laughter from my eyes.

Slade squared his stance, folded his arms, and looked me dead-on. "After careful consideration, a Band-Aid would appear to be in order." We both laughed. "Good to see ya in one piece, Wintahs. Saw your car—yikes! What happened?"

"I'm okay, Slade. I got rear-ended."

"You got more than rear-ended, from what I saw, and you saved the life of the lady that pancaked your car."

"You would have done the same thing, Slade."

"Yeah, but I didn't. *You* did, Wintahs."

"Do you know anything about her, Slade? I'm pretty certain I remember seeing her at the party."

"Good catch. You *did* see her at the party. She's Donovan Quinn's sister-in-law."

"His sister-in-law?"

"Yeah, Dane Quinn's sister."

" I had no idea."

"Yep. Her name is Kassidy Kane. Also found out that the toxicology report for her ain't gonna look so good when it comes back. I hear she was tanked."

"Yeah, I could smell the alcohol on her when I pulled her out of her car."

"She's here."

"She's *here?*"

"That's another yep, ICU. She was banged up pretty good from the impact of the airbags whackin' her in the face."

"Okay, okay. I'm going to get back to that. Can I digress?"

"Think I know where you wanna digress to. Digress away."

"What the hell happened at the Quinn residence after the party? The news report said that there was an explosion, and then a fire, and that three people died. Slade, what happened?"

"Tell ya, Wintahs, I don't know. I left that party

during the second line."

"And *we* left after the second line."

"Heard about the explosion, fire, whatever it was, 'bout the same time I heard about your accident, which wasn't 'til early this mornin'. So I don't really know much at this point, but the unofficial word is that Dane and the two youngest kids died in the fire. All I could find out was, everybody had left, and Quinn and his son were the only ones there at the time. Right now it's between the Coroner's office and the Fire Department, unless and until they deem a homicide took place."

I twisted and contorted my face as I listened closely to what Slade was telling me.

"I know that look, Wintahs. What?"

"Here's what I know, Slade. Early on that night, a while before I said 'hi' to you at the party, I thought I heard a gunshot. It was loud, and no one else seemed to have heard it, so I filed it away."

"Until now."

"Until now."

"A gunshot, through all that noise, Wintahs?"

"I'm positive. I know what I heard. I even asked Jay if he heard anything."

"Jay?"

"My date, Jay."

"Oh, yeah, Pretty Boy," Slade interrupted with a trace of laughter in his voice.

"Anyway, given the ungodly fact that three people died, and that I heard a gunshot, I'm pretty certain that a lot more is going to come out of the rubble."

"Like?"

"Like my sixth sense right now is telling me that the Fire Department will be handing the case over to you as a homicide very soon." I intensely eyeballed my friend. My heart began to palpitate a little faster as a familiar conflict of emotions took hold—the sadness over the loss of life, fused with the utter passion for finding out who and why, were in full throttle.

"Humph," Slade pensively replied, snapping me out of my thought. He folded his arms, lowered his chin, and raised his left eyebrow. "Even though the Police and Fire Department lines run deep around here, I do have a few contacts on the NOFD [New Orleans Fire Department]. Let me see what I can find out."

"Chief Wade?" I quickly asked.

"Oh, nah, Wintahs. I don't have any pull there. In fact, I got negative pull."

"How could anybody not like you, Slade?" I sarcastically asked my friend.

"Beats the hell out of me. But trust me on this one. I'm outta that loop. Unless and until they decide one or all of the deaths are homicides, it's officially a Fire Department matter. And then there's still not a guarantee that they'll turn it over to us. Anyway, one thing at a time here. Let's get *you* out of the hospital first, okay?"

Another knock on the door made itself known. "Come in!" I responded.

In walked a white-coated, round-faced man with a pleasant smile. "Dr. Winters, are you ready to go home? I'm Dr. Christian Blackwell." He splashed a stream of foam into his hands from the disinfectant mounted on the wall.

"You better believe it," I jokingly responded. "You run a lovely establishment here, but one night is more than enough."

"Now, if it's all right with you, Doctor, I'm going to take another look at that bruise on your head." Dr. Blackwell gently touched my head as he examined my abrasion. Slade and I spied each other's eyes and lightly chuckled at the good doctor's familiar technique.

"I'm thinkin', now's a good time ta' make my exit, Wintahs?" Slade interjected.

I momentarily interrupted the doctor's examination and turned toward my friend. "Okay, Slade. We'll talk later. Wait a minute, before you go—you know anything about this?" I pointed at the brown bag of clothes on the tray.

Slade gave me that crooked smile and a wink. "See ya later, Wintahs."

✦ CHAPTER 4 ✧

Why waste the blessing of a coincidence? I said to myself as I walked through the corridor of Tulane Hospital toward their intensive care unit. Discharged shortly after Dr. Blackwell's visit, I decided to pay the lady in red a visit on my way out. *This is okay,* I thought, as I looked down at the red jogging suit and sneakers I was wearing.

I tapped the 'OPEN DOOR' metal pad-button on the wall. The doors slowly parted, revealing five glassed-in ICU patient rooms in a semi-circle facing the nurse's station—an area normally quiet except for the beeps and hisses of heart-monitor and life-support machines. Today, however, it was unusually noisy. A grieving family stood inside and out of the last room to the right, sobbing, moaning and crying at what I could only assume to be the loss of their loved one. But the commotion, sad as it may have been, was a welcomed distraction as I walked around the semi-circle of rooms, opposite the grieving family.

I know she's still here, I thought as I passed two rooms, approaching the third. "That's her," I whispered in excited release, recognizing her striking features through the bruises. I stepped in. She appeared to be sleeping. She was a bit bruised and swollen, but it was her. I scanned the room: *IV, heart monitor, oximeter, oxygen, no intubation.* She wasn't on a respirator. "Excellent," I whispered.

"Kassidy?" I gently spoke, hoping to quietly awaken her, but to no avail. So I took it up a notch. "Kassidy? Can you hear me? It's Morgan Winters." I touched her hand lightly. She moaned and began to struggle to open her eyes. Once she did, I gave her a kind smile and gently squeezed her hand, hoping she would remember me. She did.

"Thank you." She barely spoke, and then closed her eyes again as a tear streamed down the side of her face.

"You're welcome. It's good to see you."

She nodded.

"I'm not going to stay long," I continued. "I know your family is thrilled that you're going to be all right, especially your sister Dane," I reluctantly added, testing the waters for a reaction, though I knew the frailty of her condition could taint her answer.

Just then though, she squeezed my hand. "Come closer."

I leaned in as close as I could to her.

"Dane is the devil," she venomously asserted in my ear.

"Excuse me, are you a family member?" went a voice from the doorway, startling me out of my trancelike preoccupation from what I had just heard from Ms. Kane.

She released my hand as I turned to face the nurse. "Oh, I'm so sorry," I quickly told her.

"Dr. Winters?"

"Yes?" I smiled in response to the nurse.

"Dr. Winters, you know the rules."

"I do. Is that 'Nurse Janna'?"

"Yes, it is."

"Please forgive me." I told her as I quickly made my way out of the room and the ward, finding it easier to apologize than to ask permission.

*   *   *   *

"Oh, Lawd, there she is! I know you said that you were all right. But ya just don't know 'til ya lay eyes on a person. It's so good ta' see ya, Doc."

"Good to see you, too, Kendall." My secretary and confidant greeted me with open arms as I walked through the front door to my office.

"Here's your coffee, and here's the chart for ya first patient."

I grabbed a seat in one of the waiting room chairs as we both sighed in momentary relaxation.

"What a weekend, huh, Doc?"

"You got that right—quite a weekend." I took a whiff and then a sip from the white mug of dark-roast chicory coffee.

"Ya doin' all right, though, huh, Doc?"

"I'm fine. A couple of bumps and bruises here and there, but I'm good."

"One thing's for sure. You doin' a lot better than that Quinn family, huh?"

"Awww, Kendall, I know."

"Yeah, Doc, it's all over the news. I even saw Lester reportin' it on the national news. Those two precious li'l children, and that pretty Miss Quinn. Terrible, just terrible how accidents happen like that, just awful." Kendall shook her head in dismay and took a sip of coffee as we sat in reflection. "Really, Doc, how does somethin' like that just happen, huh?"

"I don't know. That's a good question. How *does* something like that *just happen*?"

"Wait a minute, Doc, are you sayin' what I think you're *not* sayin'?"

In reaction, I raised my left eyebrow and twisted my mouth to the side. Kendall's eyes widened at my reply. Just then, the outer door chime went off, informing us that someone had entered the general office. "Oh, shoot! That must be Miss Ivy. She's a li'l early. But we gonna finish this, right, Doc?" Kendall put her hand around the side of her mouth to whisper to me. "My inquirin' mind wants to know."

As the visitor walked in, Kendall seamlessly switched gears from wide-eyed curiosity to congenial cheer—as only Kendall could do. "Good mornin', Miss Ivy."

"Good morning, Ivy," I said. "Right this way." I held my office door open and watched the statuesque six-foot beauty saunter past me—the first patient of the day, one Mrs. Ivy Carlisle Steele. She was always so well put together—a bit more conservative than before, though. Nonetheless, she was usually *très chic,* and today was no different. Her black-and-yellow floral print knee-length chiffon dress with black pumps complemented her flawless brown skin to perfection. She had also begun to wear a hurt-filled smile that betrayed the look of composure her image would suggest.

"Have a seat. How are you today, Ivy?" I extended

my hand to her and gestured toward the plush brown fabric sofa. As she took her seat, I sat down perpendicular to her in a black leather swivel chair and removed my Louboutins. Once we were both situated, I gave her an easy smile. The side of her mouth curved into a faint smirk that was quickly wiped away by a flood of tears.

After some fifteen minutes of sobbing, Ivy interrupted herself. "I don't know why I'm crying," she said with her British accent as she reached for a tissue from the coffee table. "I don't know why I'm here."

You know why you're crying, I thought as I sat quietly, observing and listening. *You're just not quite ready to share it with me.* Her depressed posture finally matched the distant look of sadness on her face. Her back was round, in a weighted slump. Her hands were loosely clasped together on her lap when not dabbing her tears.

"It's just so hard," she managed to speak through her sobs.

"*What's* hard, Ivy?"

"This!" She abruptly raised her left hand, flashing the ten-carat emerald-cut diamond brandishing her ring-finger. "He says that he loves me, but I've hardly seen him since we've been married. And when he's home…" Ivy dabbed away more tears from her delicately-high cheekbones.

My patient was talking about her husband of six

months. They met right after she had completed her therapeutic mandate with me for anger management some months ago. I encouraged her to continue on with therapy, but she wouldn't. She told me she was done.

The next thing I knew, the nuptials of Ivy Carlisle were being reported in the news. Two weeks ago, she had showed up at my office, newly married, distraught, sleep-deprived, and this time more passively angry than ever, clearly displaying signs of depression. This time the leggy model had come back with an added conflict of interest. Her new husband was none other than Redmann Steele, owner and CEO of Simon & Steele Publishing—my publisher. Ivy was his fourth wife. Up until today, our sessions, this go-round, had been surface-level.

"When he's home, one minute he's full of love and affection," she continued, still teary-eyed. "The next, he's raging, cruel, judgmental, and critical of my every move. He hates the way I dress. Says that I need to cover up when we're out together. I must have changed clothes five times this morning. I was almost late today, and he can't even see me. He's not even in town. This is making me crazy. Doctor, I dress the same way I've always dressed. When we were dating, he loved the fact that I was a top model. He told me that it made him feel good when we were out together. He told me that I was the best, the prettiest, the sassiest. He would pour it on, and I loved hearing that from him. We couldn't get enough of each other. We were addicted to each other."

"When did that change, Ivy?"

"Not long after saying 'I do,' it began."

"*What* began, Ivy?"

My client took an exasperated breath. "In my entire life, Doctor, I've never experienced such hurtful words. When he starts, there's no stopping him until he's said everything he knows to hurt me. There's a seemingly uncontrollable entitled rage in him."

"Give me an example, Ivy," I said, taking into account the irony of her current reality. When I first saw Mrs. Steele—back when she was Ivy Carlisle, before she was married—we had many a counseling session working through her entitled rage.

"He says things like, 'You're ignorant to matters of money, so I'll have to take care of you.' Or, 'You're just like those lame women that don't do well when they're done modeling.' I don't know how I ever managed to have a career on my own—you hear him tell it. Doctor, I've been a top model for the last ten years. I've made millions, and I *have* millions. I don't have as much as he does, but I can well take care of myself. As if all that weren't enough, whether he's away or home, he wants a full report of my whereabouts. He doesn't trust me. Yet he's never home. He does to me what I used to do to other people, but only ten times worse. He never takes the blame for anything. It's always *my* fault, whatever it is. I know I'm rambling on. This is exhausting." Ivy slumped back and exhaled.

*My patient's description of her husband, my pub-
lisher, was that of a classic self-absorbed, power-driv-
en, insecure man,* I thought as I pondered what I was
hearing from my client. *He's either projecting on to
you what he's afraid that he is, or what he's afraid he's
not.*

"I've been keeping this from everybody I know,"
Ivy continued. "Dr. Winters, I'm not perfect. I've never
claimed to be perfect. But what have I done to deserve
this? Why has love brought me here? I'm so ashamed
and embarrassed. I can't believe this is my life. This is
my dirty little secret."

Ivy began to cry again—this time, though,
gut-wrenching tears. As we sat in that moment, I noticed the intercom light flashing on my desk. *Kendall
never lights my phone up when I'm seeing a patient.
It'll have to wait,* I told myself as Ivy continued to cry.

A soft knock on the door sustained the interruption. *What is going on?* I thought as I eyed my patient.
She was so immersed in her grief that the would-be
intrusion escaped her notice. But the second knock
came harder and louder, jolting Ivy from the comfort
of the moment.

"Was that a knock?" she asked in an unsteady
whisper.

"Yes, it was, Ivy. I'm so sorry, Ivy. I'll see what Kendall wants, and I'll be right back." I slid my shoes back
on and walked out of the office, quickly closing the
door behind me. "What's going on?" I whispered to

my confidant.

"Doc," she commanded in an anxious hushed tone, "you know I never disturb you. But I jus' didn't know what ta' do. He jus' came in here and said that he needed ta' talk to you right away or he was gonna kill himself. So I got ta' buzzin' and ta' knockin.'"

Kendall widened her eyes and tilted her head toward the waiting room, where a thin, pale-complexioned young man sat. It was Aaron Quinn, son of Donovan and the late Dane Quinn. I walked over to where he was sitting.

"Hi Aaron, your appointment's not scheduled 'til next week," I cautiously addressed him, noticing the cold, distant glare of his long-lashed, bold, round eyes. "What's going on? Kendall tells me you want to see me *today.*"

He showed no outward acknowledgement of my presence. I didn't want to leave him, but I had to finish up with Ivy.

"Aaron, I'm going to need you to wait a few minutes. I'll be right back. I want to talk to you, okay? Wait right here."

He remained unresponsive, except for his eyes, which became intensely alive when he heard me say I would be "right back." He broke his empty gaze to give me a flash of irritation in his look. *So he hears me,* I thought. I lightly touched his shoulder to reassure him of my sincerity. Then I hastened my way back to

Kendall and told her in my softest voice, "I'm going to end my session with Ivy. Schedule her for the same time next week, and then I want *you* to see her to the door."

"Got it, Doc," Kendall silently mouthed to me. "Do you want me to call the police?".

"Slade," I mouthed back. Her eyebrows shot up as she nodded her head in revelatory agreement.

When I returned to my office, Ivy was standing, ready to bolt, her purse completely packed. "Ivy, I'm *so* sorry for the interruption. I see you're ready to go." By this time she had tucked away any visual traces of vulnerability that had been exposed during our session.

"Quite all right, Doctor. Like you say, things do happen for a reason, and I think I've bared enough of myself today. In fact, I'm rather embarrassed."

Her nugget of honesty demanded that I reprioritize. "Ivy, have a seat."

"But don't you have to—"

"It's okay, have a seat."

"You have nothing to be embarrassed of. The courage you've shown here today in, as you put it, exposing yourself is something for you to be proud of. Well done. We're often as sick as our darkest personal secrets and shame. You just shined a light from within onto your life."

Ivy's coat of armor began to crack again as she quickly wiped away a lone tear that managed to roll down her cheek. "Same time next week, Doctor?" she timidly spoke as I opened the door and followed behind her to see Kendall running toward the front of the office.

"Honey, wait!" Kendall yelled as the front door closed. I looked at the chair Quinn was seated in. It was empty.

"Where's..."

"He's gone, Doc," she uttered in her most dejected voice.

Dammit! I thought as Ivy clutched the strap of her purse. Her eyes darted back and forth in justified alarm. She was clearly unnerved.

"Ivy, Kendall's going to get some information from you and confirm your appointment," I coolly told her, making every attempt to project an air of calm, keeping her away from the front door until I was sure the coast was clear.

"Let's see, Miss Ivy..." Kendall said as she made her way back to her desk and I made my way toward the main entryway. My heart began to race as I reached for the doorknob. As I turned and pulled, my hand was met with a stern push from the other side. "Oh!" I yelped in surprise. I released the knob and stepped back.

"Whoa! Where ya at, there, Wintahs?" The twinkle from my cohort's calm glare through the blinding sun slowed my racing heart.

"Slade, get in here."

"What's going on? I saw the bat-signal in the sky, and came as soon as I could," he quipped in sarcasm as he walked in and looked around.

"Did you see anything strange out there?" I quietly asked.

"Just the usual. Oh, except for a guy that looked like Aaron Quinn in a sleek Mercedes screeching out of the parking lot."

"What's going on?"

"I'll explain everything in a minute. Kendall, you about done over there?" I yelled to my secretary to let her know the coast was clear.

"All done, Doc. We'll see you next week, okay, Miss Ivy?"

"Very well."

"Okay Ivy, next week, same time—and, please, remember what I told you."

She coyly looked into my eyes and nodded in the affirmative.

As we walked past Slade and out the front door, I surveyed the area. I didn't see anything out of the ordinary, but there was something. My periphery caught a glimpse of a familiar shadowed likeness of a man on foot. He had turned the corner before I could clearly focus in on him. It wasn't Aaron. He was gone.

"Humph!" I exclaimed as I watched Ivy get into her Alfa Romeo and close the door. I took a deep breath, turned around, and zeroed in on Slade. "Good to see you, partner."

"Always good to see you, Wintahs, but what's going on? By the way, wasn't that the super-model Ivy Carlisle?"

I gestured for Slade to sit in one of the waiting-room chairs. I sat next to him, slid my pumps off, and began to rub the back of my neck. "Can't answer that first question," I told him. "You know why. But I can tell you that you did see Aaron Quinn here."

"Okay, so, then, what's the deal with Aaron Quinn?

"He stopped by a little while ago and insisted on seeing me..."

"Commanda,'" Kendall interjected, "he said that if he didn't see Doc he was gonna kill himself. Sho' as I tell ya. That's what he said. Oh, I'm sorry, Doc. He got me all flustered, comin' in here like that." She shook her head.

"It's okay, I'm a little flustered, too," I told my secretary as I turned toward Slade to observe the movement of his eyebrows, seeking validation of Kendall's account.

"Just like she said," I assured him. "He just showed up, demanded to see me, and used his own life as a bargaining tool. I only saw him for a minute, though. I was in the middle of a session. Kendall knocked on the door. I came out, and he was sitting right there where you're sitting."

"And, Commanda', if he said one word, he said a lot, after he threatened to take his life," Kendall chimed in.

"Nothing, huh?" Slade asked.

"Nothing," I said. "I asked him to sit tight until I was done with my patient. But he wouldn't even look at me, except for one brief moment. But I know he heard me."

"How's that?" Slade asked.

Kendall squinted her eyes and tilted her head to the side, honing in on what I was about to say: "He rolled his eyes and looked off to the side in irritation when I told him I had a patient, and that I couldn't talk to him right away. He heard me."

"Can I tell it from here, Doc?"

"Take it away."

"Well, Commanda', Doc went in ta' see her patient. I went ova' and asked Mr. Quinn if I could get him some coffee or water or somethin', 'cause, between the three of us, he was lookin' a li'l like death warmed ova'. He didn't look so good. What did I ask that for? That boy turned and looked at me, with eyes as big as my fist. He clutched the arms of that chair." She pointed to the chair Slade was sitting in and then gripped the arms of her chair. "And he sent pure devilment through that look he gave me. Oh, Lawd, y'all, and I just let his anger go right through me. Mother Franklin..."

Kendall took a breath and then paused as she reverently looked toward the heavens. "Mother Franklin would always say, 'Don't you let somebody else's monkey get on your back. 'Cause somebody else's monkey ain't nothin' but fear lookin' for a new home.' Amen!" Kendall looked at Slade and me for an endorsement.

"Amen," Slade quickly added, once he realized she was done.

"Anyway, like I was sayin', before I knew it, him and his anger got up and just walked on outta here. I didn't know what to do. I wanted to just start yellin', 'Doc, get out here! He's leavin'! He's leavin'!' Couldn't do that, though. So I just kinda' followed afta' him. But he was gone like the wind."

As Kendall continued to recall what happened, I took a moment to steal a peek at Slade. In what was only supposed to be a glance, I found my eyes loitering as I watched him rub his ruggedly commanding chin. *I really like him, I might even...Oh no!* I thought as he caught me and winked one of his deep-set brown eyes before I could look away. *Damn that Slade.*

Kendall finished her account, none the wiser of the interaction between Slade and me: "And the next thing ya know, Doc and Miss Ivy were comin' out of the office."

"He didn't say anything?" Slade asked.

"Nada, zippo, zilch, nothing! It was so quiet in here, as Mother Franklin used ta' say, you could hear the roaches talkin'."

Slade and I were silent. *That's a new one*, I thought.

"Anyway, Slade," I said, signaling with my forefinger to draw his attention back. "I'm certain it's not a coincidence that he showed up here a couple of days after his mother and two siblings died in a house fire. He's reaching out. Very sorry that I couldn't talk to him. But that's kind of how life is. Right?"

"Absolutely. Gotta ask ya this, Wintahs."

"Go ahead."

"Is he one of your patients?"

"Yes, he *is* one of my patients. And the minute he threatened to take his life, released me from any professional, ethical, or personal conflict, in regards to revealing information about his visit. It then became my responsibility to call the authorities, hence, the call to you, Commander Slade. I just started seeing him a few weeks ago. Let me give you a little history on young Mr. Quinn. He came to see me for stealing."

"Stealing?"

"Yes, stealing. It was a therapy sentence instead of a jail sentence. He presented with addictive compulsive stealing. The first time I saw him, he was full of gut-wrenching shame and guilt. He hung his head, had little or no eye contact at all. But he managed to talk about his anger-driven urges to steal. Today was different, though, like Kendall said. He showed up at the office threatening to either see me or take his life. And when I couldn't see him right away, at first he pouted, then ran off, like children do when they don't get their way."

"Oh, I know that look, Wintahs—folding your arms, index-finger over your mouth. What's going on up there?"

"That young man is a ticking bomb," I told Slade point-blankly.

"Jus' waitin' ta' go off, huh, Doc?" Kendall said.

I raised my eyebrows in agreement.

"I don't know about anybody else, but I could use a nice cup a' hot tea. Doc? Commanda'?" Kendall offered.

"I would love a cup of tea," I replied.

"What about you, Commanda'?"

"I'm good, Kendall." Slade gave her the thumbs-up sign.

"I would love to get ahold of any official information of any kind about what happened at the Quinn residence the night of the fire," I told Slade. "Is there any way I can—and when I say 'I,' I mean 'you.' " I pointed at him. "Can you get your hands on some sort of preliminary incident report? Is there such a thing with the Fire Department?"

Slade twisted his mouth, sat back in his chair, folded his arms, and put his hand over his chin in thought.

"Look at him think, Doc," Kendall added, chuckling at her own commentary.

"Let me think about it, Wintahs."

"Oh, shoot, Doc, here comes your next appointment," Kendall interrupted. "I just love watchin' you and the Commanda' in action."

"All right, I'm gonna take that as my cue to roll up on outta here," Slade announced. "I'm supposed to be meetin' a friend for lunch in a few." He looked at his watch.

Wonder if he's seeing his date from the party.

"I'll let ya know what I find out about gettin' a hold of a fire incident report," he told me.

"Thanks, Slade. What's your schedule like tomorrow evening?"

"What do ya have?"

"I'm one of the presenters at the UNO [University

of New Orleans] mental health lecture series. It starts at six. Any chance that you're free? Oh, yeah, before you say no, guess who else is slated to be there?"

"Who?"

"Donovan Quinn."

"Really?"

"Yeah, he was supposed to be speaking on what it takes to 'fix your life,' the title of his new book."

"Surprised he's still doin' it."

"Yeah, me, too. I presume this was planned way before the fire. What do you say? It's a student event, no dress code, and it'll give us a chance to talk afterwards."

"Where's it gonna be?" he coolly asked.

"UNO's Hitt Alumni center."

"I'll be there. Kinda' like hearing *your* lectures, Wintahs." Slade turned around, holding me still with his eyes. "Oh, and by the way, she's prettier in person."

"Who? Oh." I quickly smiled at my friend's not-so-subtle acknowledgement of his recognition of my patient, Ivy Carlisle-Steele.

"Y'all be careful. Don't want anything happenin' to anybody around here, okay?"

"We're good, Slade. Thanks, and see you tomorrow."

❧ CHAPTER 5 ❧

I stepped out of the shower and grabbed a towel from the towel warmer. The heated cloth wrapped around my bare chocolate-chip-brown skin was the next best thing to a hug, after a long day. "Ahhh, so nice," I said out loud as the sound of my cellphone ringing broke my entrancement. I scurried off to my bedroom, picked up the phone, and flopped across my bed. "Jay," the name said on the caller ID.

"Hello, Beautiful," his smooth baritone voice greeted me on the other end of the phone.

"Hi, Jay. How are you?"

" 'How are you' is the *question*. How was your day?"

"It was decent," I replied as my mind flashed back to Aaron Quinn, and then Slade being in my office.

"What about you? How was *your* day?"

"My day was good, Morgan. But the more important question here is, when can I see you again? I know you're a busy woman, Doctor, but you have to take a break some time. How about lunch?"

"I would love to, Jay. When and where?"

"Music to my ears, Morgan. How about Willie Mae's Scotch House, on..."

"On St. Ann, right?"

"On St. Ann. How about Thursday? Around noon good for you?"

"Noon is perfect."

"Well, all right, Morgan Winters, I'll see you Thursday. You sleep tight, okay?"

"I will. Good night, Jay."

I rolled onto my stomach and reached for the TV remote with every intention of turning to QVC, but the *Ten O'Clock News'* lead story halted my progress.

"That's right, Nancy, we can now confirm that one of the three bodies found in that awful house fire in Algiers Point was that of Dane Quinn," said the news anchor. "She is said to have been shot in the head prior to the fire. We contacted the New Orleans Police Department, and they released this statement:

" 'The house fire and the deaths of Donovan Jr.,

Ashleigh, and Dane Quinn are part of an active and ongoing investigation. We continue to consider all forensic and investigative information as it pertains to this tragic occurrence. The New Orleans Police Department is committed to finding the person or persons responsible for this horrific crime. With that, we ask that anyone who has any information about the fire and/or the deaths of these three people, please come forward.'

"That's it from Algiers Point. Back to you, Nancy."

I muted the TV. "I knew it," I said with an exasperated sigh.

❧ CHAPTER 6 ❧

"Merriam-Webster defines 'guilt' as 'bad feelings caused by knowing or thinking that you've done something wrong or bad.' Webster defines 'shame' as 'a painful emotion caused by consciousness of guilt, shortcoming, or impropriety.' Today I want to challenge what a lot of us have been taught to believe about these two words, 'guilt' and 'shame.'"

I paused for a moment, removed my glasses, and took a good look at the audience of young adults. "When one feels guilt, he or she is usually motivated to do what?" I asked the crowd.

"Confess!" a shoulder-length brown-haired young man shouted out from the middle of the auditorium.

"Yes! What else?"

"Ask for forgiveness!" another shouted.

"Yes, ask for forgiveness! So, we can say that a large part of guilt is embedded in how we feel about what we've done to someone else, right? Let's do the same thing for shame. When one feels shame, he or she is motivated to do what?" I once again peered out into the sea of attendees.

"Apologize," a couple volunteered. "Ask forgiveness."

"It's the same as guilt, right?" a petite blond in the front row shouted out.

"You all agree?"

Many of the attendees nodded in agreement. As I scanned the room again for a brief moment, I saw the same shadowy figure of a man from my office appear and then vanish through one of the exits. I made as much as I could of a mental note of what I had just seen, took a sip of water, and refocused.

"Does anybody disagree?"

Silence permeated the room.

"Well, then, here lies the challenge of a different way of thinking. No, it's not the same. Shame will motivate you to hide, lie, cheat, and maybe even kill. But it will not motivate you to apologize or ask for forgiveness. Shame will also encourage you to blame others for your bad behavior or isolate yourself, in your shame. Shame is that dull ache in the pit of your stomach that tells you you're alone in your imperfection, or sin. You're not good enough. 'Something about me doesn't belong here, or there.' It makes you want to hide. And then, after you've appropriately isolated yourself by making your sin a secret, it'll invite depression, or food, drugs or a bottle to the party. Shame, real shame, is to be revealed, talked about, confronted, and then excavated. I'll say this again: Shame will never motivate you to apologize or ask for forgiveness!

"The guilt-ridden man says, 'What I did to him, or to her, or to them, was awful or bad.' The shame-filled man says, '*I* am bad' or '*I* am awful because of what I've done.' Do you see the difference?"

The room murmured in contemplation as I went on. "We're learning now that shame may be at the root of many of our societal ills—suggesting that, at the core of addiction, domestic abuse, bullying, and, yes, even murder, is oftentimes deep-seeded self-reproach, self-hate, insecurity, shame."

I stopped for a moment to take a sip of water from the bottle sitting on the podium. *It's now or never, Morgan,* I told myself as uneasiness set in at the thought of going off-script and speaking publically about my own shame. *Nope, not today*, I frustratingly thought, and went on with the planned lecture....

Some twenty minutes later: "Here's the big take-home today. I'd like all of you in earshot—and I mean *all* of you—" I scanned the room and caught sight of Slade in the back. *When did he get here?* I wondered. I continued: "I want you to ask yourselves, 'What am I holding on to, masking, or hiding, that may be causing me to doubt who I am, causing me to believe that I am less than the person I was put here to be?' "

I paused again to absorb the pensive energy of the quiet auditorium. "And let's be honest. A lot of what I'm talking about can fall under the umbrella of that stigmatic phrase of 'mental illness.' Even we mental health professionals can fall prey to secrecy and feelings of shame when it comes to our mental health. There is no shame in admitting you have a problem. There is no shame in seeking help. There is only redemption, resurrection, and freedom of the mind, body, and spirit. Once you've revealed whatever that *thing* is to yourself, start the excavation process. *Call it out!*" I exclaimed with authority. "Cut it off at the knees, and then tell somebody you trust about it. You don't have to be a victim of your past, your secrets, your pain, or your sin. They don't define who you are." I leaned into the microphone. "Stop hiding and seek the truth. Seek *your* truth. Thank you so much for listening. Until the next time, guys."

I picked up my bottle of water and left the podium. The applause continued as I made my way off to the side and toward the rear of the auditorium.

"Thank you, Dr. Winters, for that thought-provoking and honest lecture," the facilitator remarked as the applause went on. "Come back out here, Doctor, and take another bow."

I made my way back to the podium as the crowd continued to clap and cheer. It felt great that they seemed to hear what I was saying. *Maybe the next time I'll be able to give them the full speech,* I thought. *Physician, heal thyself.* "Thank you, thank you," I told them as the plaudits began to taper off their clapping.

"Our next speaker, renowned author of *You Can Do it, One More Time, It's All Up To You, Yes You Can,* and his latest, *Fix Your Life,* Donovan Quinn, is here tonight. He's traveled the world as a lecturer, and motivational speaker..."

"You never cease to amaze me, Wintahs," Slade whispered in my ear as Quinn's introduction continued. "Good stuff."

"How much did you hear?" I asked him.

"Everything." He looked me in the eye.

Again, his lady friend showed up out of nowhere, this time with a couple of cellphones and a clipboard. "Hi again, Dr. Winters," she said. "Can I just tell you that was awesome? Every word hit home. We all have secrets, right?"

"Absolutely, Ms. Mendez, absolutely."

"I have to get back to Dr. Quinn. But it was great seeing you again, Dr. Winters. Jackie, we'll talk later, right?"

Slade gave Ms. Mendez a soft salute, as she smiled and left his side. The sting from seeing her again wasn't so intense this time. We listened to the rest of Donovan's introduction.

"...And, might I add..." The announcer lowered her voice in reverence. "We are so grateful to Dr. Quinn for honoring his commitment to be here, in spite of the terrible loss he and his family suffered. So, without further ado, let's welcome author, educator and motivational speaker Donovan Quinn."

The tall, dark-haired, alabaster-complexioned lecturer walked up to the podium amid boisterous applause. "Good evening, young people," he began with a smile. "Good evening. Oh, and I see some not-so-young folks out there as well. Good evening, all."

A few snickered as Quinn took a sip of water. "As Dr. Smith mentioned, I—"

CLAP-CLAP-CLAP-CLAP-CLAP went someone from the rear of the auditorium in the shadows. The room began to murmur in disturbed curiosity as the clapping continued.

"I see we have someone who's heard me speak before and can't contain themselves,"

Donovan humorously said in an attempt to relax the atmosphere as well as quiet the heckler.

"Donovan Quinn, Dr. Quinn, famed novelist and lecturer, what should I call you?" inquired a voice from the dark.

"Oh, boy," I said out loud. Even though the commotion had come from the other side of the auditorium, I recognized the voice of the agitator.

"What? Who is that?" Slade quickly asked.

"I'm here to fix our lives, Dad. It's the family business, right?" shouted Aaron Quinn, as he appeared from the shadows.

"Oh," Slade realized.

"What are you doing, Aaron? Don't do this," Donovan pleaded.

"Don't do what? Oh, oh, that's right, not in public, huh?" Aaron chuckled, then summarily tightened his lips and sternly looked at his father. "Not today, Dad. For once, a member of the Quinn family—what's left of us—is going to tell the truth."

The senior Quinn made a move toward his son. "Come on, son, let's handle this at home."

"Get away from me!" Aaron shrieked and jerked away as stunned attendees continued to watch in alarm. "At home? Since *when* do we talk at home? We don't talk at home. We don't talk anywhere. But you know what? Today's a new day for the Quinn family." Aaron paused for a moment to look around the room. "No more secrets, Dad, no more. Mother told me that she would just as soon die than air the family's dirty laundry. Humph, funny how things happen, huh?" Aaron's eyes went cold and he stared off for a moment. "I guess it's *not* so funny, huh? Go figure—your brother, sister and mother die, and your dad's still working twenty-four-seven, just like nothing ever happened. You know what? I lived my life trying not to be a disappointment to you and mother. I managed to screw that up, didn't I? If the memory of my life serves me correct, I've been a disappointment to you since I was born. Haven't I, Dad?"

Quinn's expression went from complete fear and anguish to one of puzzlement. "You don't have to pretend anymore. I'm going to set both of us free, today. That's right, I know. Mother told me the night of the party. She seemed to get a sick enjoyment from it. She said that it was time that I knew."

Aaron pointedly looked into his father's eyes. A moment of revelation with frozen shock appeared to reign clear in the senior Quinn's face. "I know you're not my father. I know we don't share the same DNA. I know that it wasn't my paranoid imagination, like you and Mother used to tell me, that I was treated differently."

"Son, I'm your dad. I'm going to *always* be your dad. Come on, let's go home. We were only trying to protect you."

"You *weren't* trying to protect me. You were trying to protect *yourselves* and your precious image. I was the last thing on your mind. It's too late for that anyway."

Aaron reached into the pocket of his denim jacket and removed a shiny black pistol. The spectators squawked and squealed in terror, scrambling for a way out of the room. Sweat was now trickling down Donovan's panic-stricken forehead.

"I don't suppose it'll do any good for me to tell ya to get outta here, will it, Wintahs?" Slade whispered into my ear as he drew his own weapon. I momentarily looked away from Aaron and his father to shoot my friend a deadpan look of incredulity at his question.

"So what's the plan?" I whispered back.

"Wintahs, let me handle this one," Slade pointlessly suggested as the tumult continued and the younger Quinn went on.

"No need to worry, people!" he shouted to the swarming students. "Today is about me and my dad, or Donovan, or Dr. Quinn, or whoever he is." He turned to his father. "I don't know what to call you anymore, man. But I do know that I won't be disappointing you anymore. No more disappointment. Remember this?"

The younger Quinn looked longingly at the black pistol in his hand, and then pointed it at his own temple as his father stared back at him in incredulous silence. "You gave this nine millimeter to me after Kenny," Aaron continued. "Remember my best friend Kenny, Dad? You stood there while mother told me that the two of you thought I'd like to have one like him. Y'all told me that right after I found out he blew his brains away. I was eleven years old. Why would you do that Dad? I was so confused. But you know what? I'm not confused anymore."

Aaron's voice went cold, his face expressionless. "One for me, and one for you," he emotionlessly asserted. "Bullets—one bullet for me, and one bullet for you." He pointed the gun at himself and then at his father.

"We didn't mean to hurt you, son," the senior Quinn timorously pleaded. "We made some mistakes. But it's going to be okay, though. Just give me the gun, son." He once again attempted to approach Aaron.

The younger Quinn continued on as his sad, drawn eyes looked back at the empty auditorium. "They're all gone. I guess it's just you and me."

"That's right, son. It's just you and me. You don't have to do this. Just put the gun down."

"I told you to be quiet. Please, just be quiet. I'm tired. I'm so tired. I just want the pain to stop. I just want it to stop." Aaron's voice quivered in emotional weakness. He seemed disoriented as he rubbed his eyes and scanned the voided space.

Suddenly, a loud crackle from Slade's malfunctioning radio decided to make an appearance. "Crap," Slade whispered as he made a mad dash to restrain his police radio.

"Who's there?" Aaron nervously yelled out. Slade was still attempting to quiet his device.

"It's me, Aaron," I yelled out.

"Who?"

"Dr. Winters, Aaron. It's me."

"Wintahs, get back here," Slade demanded in a hushed tone I ignored as I maneuvered away from his fleeting attempt to hold me in place.

"It's me, Aaron." I said as I walked out into the open.

"Dr. Winters?" young Quinn asked.

"Yes it's me. Dr. Winters."

"Finally you have time for me." He painfully spoke through his now-pale lips as he turned toward me. Donovan took another hopeful step toward his son. "No!" Aaron cried out, as he pointed the gun at his father again, glancing back and forth at the two of us with detached, unyielding eyes.

"Aaron!" I loudly spoke, interrupting his mania. "You're right. I have time for you now." I noticed Slade in my periphery, making his way around to the other side of the auditorium.

"What do you want, Doctor?" the younger Quinn desperately asked.

"I just want to talk to you, Aaron," I said to him as I looked into his weary eyes. "I can see you're in pain."

"I'm just so tired, Doctor. I just want it to stop. I want all the pain to stop." Aaron hung his head, but maintained the barrel of the gun at his father.

"I'm so sorry you're hurting so much, Aaron," I said as I walked closer to him. "Look at me Aaron."

He despondently watched at his father. "Look at me." I gently asked him to do again. He slowly turned his head and locked a remote gaze on my eyes. "I'm so sorry you're hurting." I continued to walk closer, without breaking eye contact. "And I'm so sorry you had to go through all of that. It doesn't seem fair, but it's over now. All that's over now."

His dark and angry mood seemed to shift, leaving a veil of sadness over his face. I was now standing less than two feet away from the reluctant gunman.

"I'm sorry so many people hurt you, Aaron." I gently touched his shoulder and placed my other hand on top of his gun-holding hand. His body grew limp as he lowered the weapon to his side and let it fall onto the floor.

Just then, Slade appeared and kicked the gun away. "Hands up, Junior! Hands up!" he shouted at the troubled young man.

Aaron complied, with no struggle.

"Everybody okay?" yelled five or so police officers as they burst into the auditorium, guns drawn.

"You okay, Wintahs?" Slade asked me as he hand-cuffed Aaron.

"I'm good." My heart began to race at the sight of the pistol on the floor and the thought of what had just taken place.

"Yeah, guys," said Slade. "Everybody's okay. Read

'im his rights and take him downtown. I'll be right be-hind ya."

"Son, I'm sorry!" Donovan yelled from a distance as the officers led the disturbed young man out of the auditorium.

Slade and I watched from a safe distance. He turned toward me. "Wintahs?"

"Yeah, Slade?" I returned his gaze.

"I know you're good at what you do, but..." He paused.

"But what?" I noticed a look of contemplative concern in his eyes.

"But nothing. Just be careful."

"I always am, my friend." I lightly touched his hand. We smiled at each other in mutual relief and affection.

"So much for an easy evening, huh? Ya know we're gonna have to postpone our powwow."

"Yeah, I know."

"Duty and paperwork are callin'. Look at Quinn over there. Why don't you go over before they start questionin' him? See what'cha can get out of him."

Donovan was quietly sitting in the first row of seats with his head in his hands. Everyone else but the police had gone.

"There you go again, reading my mind." I gave my partner a nod and left his side. Then I walked over to Quinn and took a seat next to him.

"Doing okay, Donovan?" I asked.

He lifted his head and looked straight ahead. "I'll be fine, Morgan, I'm going to do whatever I can to help him. I don't want to lose another child. He's my son." He turned to me and looked into my eyes. "I can't believe this is happening. I can't believe my little Donnie Jr. and Ashley are gone. I can't believe..." Quinn held back tears as emotion began to choke his voice. "I can't believe this is happening. It's not supposed to be like this."

Two police officers walked up to us. "Excuse us, Dr. Winters, but we're going to need to talk to Dr. Quinn here," said one of them, who shifted his gaze to Donovan. "Sir we're going to need to get a statement from you."

Donovan cleared his throat and adjusted his demeanor. "I'll be right there. I'll see you later, Morgan."

"I'm just a phone call away, Donovan." I sincerely offered as he walked away with the officers. *He's hurting,* I thought.

I saw Slade standing with a group of officers, and we met eyes. I subtly shrugged my shoulders in resignation. He left the group and sat next to me. "Anything?" he asked.

"Just a lot of hurt."

"Tell ya what, Wintahs. How about lunch tomorrow at Bud's Broiler? I'm gonna be here a while."

"Sounds good."

✥ CHAPTER 7 ✥

"Name?" went the emotionless female voice from behind the fortified Plexiglas window.

"Dr. Winters."

"Who are you here to see?"

"Aaron Quinn."

I was at St. Paul's Mental Health facility, where they often sent the fortunate—or, rather, the wealthy few—for criminal behavior instead of Orleans Parish Prison. Though I had seen Aaron a couple of times, I wasn't officially his doctor, and I didn't know if they would let me see him. So I arrived at seven a.m. and walked in as if I belonged there.

"Ma'am, I don't see your name on the list." My stomach knotted a little as the serious woman told me what I already knew. *Here we go,* I thought.

"You're not *going* to see my name on the list," I said with a confident false bravado as I flashed my Special Investigations badge.

She scrutinized the hardware in my hand, looked me in the eye, and then looked back at the badge. "You're that crime shrink, aren't you?"

I gave the woman a humble smile.

"Through the double doors and to your right. Take the elevator to the third floor. Punch in this code." She handed me a small piece of paper with four numbers written on it. "He's in Room 307."

"Thank you," I gratefully responded, and then swiftly headed for the double doors. I wasn't sure whether it was my badge, my name, or God that got me in, but at this point it didn't matter. I was in.

The space beyond the elevator on the third floor was eerie and quiet. A fortified brown metal door with a small barred window greeted me as I stepped into the area. *There's the keypad,* I said to myself as I approached the door and peeped into its slight window. I couldn't see much. I took the piece of paper out of my pocket and punched its numbers, 1980, into the keypad. Nothing happened. I punched them in again, this time pressing the pound sign afterward. A loud buzz sounded, triggering the lock.

"Halfway there," I whispered to myself as I entered the ward and proceeded down the corridor, "304...305...306...307! There it is!"

Now, one more small favor from you God, I prayed as I approached Room 307 and reached for its doorknob. The door was unlocked. "Yes!" I whispered as I quickly opened the door and entered the room.

Sure enough, there he was, handcuffed to the metal railing of the bed. His long frame appeared frail and almost lifeless as he lay there with his eyes closed. His deep breathing was the only sign of life in the cold, aseptic room. I tiptoed closer to his bed. Suddenly, his eyes opened. They were bloodshot—full of fatigue and sadness.

"Hi," I softly spoke.

He stared right through me.

"Aaron."

"I don't want to talk," his distant, weak voice responded as he maintained his vacuous stare, eventually turning his head away. "I told the police that I don't want to talk to anybody."

"The police didn't send me. They have no idea I'm here. I understand if you don't want to talk. You don't have to. But will you listen? If you don't want to, I'll leave, Aaron."

Seconds that felt like minutes passed as he finally turned his head back around. Without words, his hurt-filled eyes broke the silence, granting me permission to speak. I knew that I had to choose my words carefully, and that there was a good chance he would not want to talk. But nothing beats failure like a good try.

So I began to talk to the pained young man with a simple truth: "I want you to know that you're not alone. No matter what, know that you are not alone." I approached him close enough to place my hand on top of his shackled hand. "No matter what you did yesterday, no matter what you've ever done, you are not alone in this world, and you are loved, Aaron."

His eyes filled with tears, and he looked away. But then he quickly turned back around. "If I'm not alone and I'm so loved, why were my brother and sister killed in a fire? Huh? Why? Why are my miserable excuses for parents able to perpetrate the scam of the century on everybody they come in contact with, and I'm in here? If I'm so loved, why is this my life?"

He held his fettered hands in the air as high as he could, while looking at me grasping for refuge in my eyes. I couldn't give it to him.

"I can't answer any of those questions, Aaron, but what I can tell you is this. The answers, the shelter, the peace you're looking for, are all locked away inside of you. And only you hold the key."

I paused, maintaining placid eye contact, hoping my words would resonate with the troubled young man. After a few moments, I continued: "From what I can see, you've been trying to do life on your own for quite some time. You don't have to do that anymore, Aaron. You're not alone, and you don't have to do that anymore."

His pleading stare began to morph into sadness as a hot tear rolled down his cheek. My anxious mind pressed, *He's ripe for the picking, Morgan. Take him. Start the interrogation,* I urged myself, but then, *Awww, damn.* I looked into his desperate eyes and realized that my heart wouldn't allow me to push any further. *Remember the oath, Morgan, 'Do no harm.'*

I took a subtle but deep breath as the quiet in the room grew noticeably loud. Suddenly, though, just as I was becoming willing to leave empty-handed, Aaron broke his silence: "My mother and father have everybody fooled. Nobody else saw what I saw." He looked off at a distance.

"What did you see, Aaron?" He slowly turned back toward me, but this time his face was full of darkness and burning animus. His eyes blazed with anger. His lips pressed tightly together. *I've seen that look before,* I thought, noticing his sudden change in disposition. *This is the man that was going to kill his father.*

"Let Aunt Kassidy tell you what was going on. 'Cause I'm done." The younger Quinn balled his hand into a fist and pulled it away from mine as much as the restraints would allow, and then looked the other way.

*   *   *   *

"'Mornin', Doc. How you doin'?" Kendall greeted me as I entered my office.

"I'm good," I said. "Had a busy night, but all's well. How are you?"

"Oh, you know me, Doc. I'm fine as a glass a' wine in the sunshine. But did I here ya say ya had a busy night?"

"Yes, you did."

"Did your busy night have somethin' to do with that lecture you had at UNO? I saw Nancy on the news talkin' about somethin' that happened there, but I didn't hear the whole story. Did somethin' happen there, Doc?" Kendall asked in a squeal of a voice, as she handed me a cup of coffee and the chart of the day's first patient.

"Something happened, all right." I lifted the white coffee mug up to my nose as I savored the rich smell of Arabica beans before taking a sip.

"What happened?"

"Kendall, the same troubled young man that stopped by here yesterday pulled a gun on his father in the middle of his lecture."

"That young Aaron Quinn?"

"Yes, Aaron Quinn pulled a gun on his father, Donovan. After he pulled the gun, he told everybody in the room in no uncertain terms that he was going to put a bullet in his father's head, as well as his own."

"Donovan Quinn? Get out and shut the front door! No he didn't!"

Too much, I thought as I enjoyed my secretary's colorful reaction to the news. "Needless to say, no shots fired," I continued. "Before you knew it, Aaron was being handcuffed and escorted out the building. Slade was there."

"Good day in the mornin', Doc! You'd just said that he was a tickin' time bomb, and look what happened. Bet you were glad that Commander Slade was there. Isn't he somethin' else? I miss seein' him around here like before."

I do, too. I thought. "Yes he is something else, one of a kind."

"But what about Dr. Quinn? Did ya get a chance to talk to him? How was he? Bet he was an upset mess, huh, Doc?"

"Yes, he was. But I didn't get a real chance to talk to him. He was busy giving statements to the police."

"Just as sure as I know that water clears up after the mud settles, I know that you're gonna get down to the bottom of all of this. Because we both know that somethin's rotten in Denmark, over there at the Quinn house." Kendall nodded her head in agreement with herself.

"Thank you for the vote of confidence."

"You're welcome, Doc. Just tellin' it like it is. And here comes your nine o'clock. Oh, wait a minute, Doc. Is that—"

"I think it is."

"Why, good mornin', Miss Ivy! Don't you look pretty! And good mornin' to you, too, Mr. Steele! I don't believe we've met before, but I recognize you from the magazines. I'm Kendall Grahm, if you know me from back-a-town, but I'm Kendall Roy, if you know me from the Bywater. That's my husband's name— Ryder Trevah Roy. But I guess it don't make no never-mind with you, cause we jus' meetin', huh? Oh, don't mind me. Today's one of those days I jus' say whatevah comes to my mind."

One of those days, otherwise known as a Wednesday, I chuckled to myself.

"Good morning—Mrs. Roy? Is it?" Redmann Steele asked as he and his wife stood in front of Kendall's desk.

"That's right. Kendall G. Roy, Mr. Steele. And how y'all doin' today?"

"Doing well, Kendall," Ivy responded.

"Well, good morning, the two of you," I greeted the stately-looking couple. "What a surprise."

Redmann stood in front of his wife in a well-tailored black suit with his signature power royal blue tie.

"Good morning. Doctor. Redmann thought that maybe he could—" Ivy nervously began.

Her husband put his hand up. "I can speak for myself." His words were sharp, and his smile was disingenuous. "I told my wife I wanted to sit in on one of these sessions with you. I didn't think you would mind."

Steele's voice was deep and impressive. My instinct was to insist that we make another appointment for a joint visit. *But this is too good,* I said to myself as I relished the thought of seeing their marital dynamic up close and personal. I was pretty certain he would never agree to an official visit. *What I know of Redmann Steele, the publisher, tells me he is used to being in control. And the little I know about Redmann Steele, the husband, tells me the same.*

"We generally like to plan this kind of visit ahead of time, Redmann, but since you're here, welcome. Come on into my office." I held my door open for the couple. Kendall and I exchanged raised eyebrow glances as they walked by.

"Both of you can sit on the couch, right there." I gestured toward the sofa. "And, Redmann, I like to get comfortable in here, so I usually take my shoes off. But don't let that throw you off. I do some of my best work in my bare feet."

I smiled at the tycoon, and then at Ivy, as I observed their demeanor. *Her legs were wrapped around each other, locked at the ankles, hands tight-*

ly clasped together on her lap. He's got the old figure four-leg clamp going—one leg crossed over the other in a sideways fashion, hands holding onto the leg on top. Usually means that he's ready to discard any view that doesn't look or sound like his. Give him a chance, Morgan. They're clearly both afraid. She's afraid of him, and he's afraid of being exposed in here.

"How are the two of you today?" I pleasantly smiled at the pair.

"I'm well, Doctor," Ivy meekly replied. She was quite different in his presence.

"And you, Redmann?"

"I'm doing great, Morgan," the tycoon overconfidently replied, with a stern smile.

"Well, then, Mr. and Mrs. Steele, why are you here today?"

Redmann's smile left his face. He took a deep, irritated breath and rolled his eyes. Ivy nervously looked away. I continued to observe the two and waited for an answer.

"I just wanted to see what goes on in here," Steele finally blurted.

"Oh, okay. Well, you're sitting in here today as Mr. and Mrs. Steele. Are you here for help for you marriage?" I asked, making note of, but outwardly ignoring, Redmann's comment.

In that moment of pause, Ivy began to shake her foot and dart her eyes about in nervous discomfort.

Her husband took another agitated breath. "Look... I just wanted to come down here and sit in on one of these sessions. You do whatever it is that you and Ivy do. Ivy said it was okay. Right?" He looked at his wife with a clenched jaw and widened eyes, passively demanding agreement. She glanced at him, but then quickly averted her eyes.

"Redmann," I interjected, "that's not how we do things in here. You and I can meet and talk, or, as I've been doing with Ivy, she and I can continue to meet and talk, or the three of us can meet together and talk about relationship matters. But you will not be observing my counseling sessions with Ivy, your wife."

He huffed and puffed in clearly entitled, frustrated annoyance. He was not happy.

His wife broke her silence and meekly suggested, "Redmann, maybe we can talk about our relationship."

"I'm not here to talk about us or me," he shot back, in callus anger. "You're the crazy one with the problems, in need of a shrink.".

"Redmann, please, calm down." Ivy touched his hand.

"Don't tell me what to do! I can't stand that about you, Ivy. That's exactly what I can't stand. You're always trying to control me. Don't tell me what to do. You're a manipulative, controlling..."

"Stop right there, Redmann," I intervened, acting on my number-one rule.

"Excuse me?" he snapped back. "Don't forget who you're talking to, Morgan. You're under contract with Simon & Steele, and I'm Steele." He turned back toward me and locked his dark eyes onto mine.

Oh my, that's intense, I thought of his now aggressive attempt to intimidate me. *I'm not in the mood for this. He wants a fight. And if that's what he wants, he's met his match today. Wait a minute, Morgan.* I wanted to strike back in kind, but the adult in me pulled rank. *Look at him. Pursed lips, flared nostrils. Mood gone from zero to a hundred in nothing flat. He's a controlling jerk. And this is how jerks behave when they don't get their way—like children. Take it down a notch, Morgan. Okay, the more useful thought is, clinically Steele presents today with what appears to be stunted emotional growth. He would love to feed off of my anger right now. Not today, buddy. You're going to have to get if from somewhere else.*

I took a deep but subtle breath and braced myself for what I was about to say to my client's husband.

"Just a minute, Redmann," I spoke directly but calmly. "Perhaps you lost sight of the fact that you're in my office. I'm not in yours. And I need to inform you of one very important rule I have." My words seemed to interrupt his tantrum as he sat back, folded his arms, crossly rolled his eyes, and sulked like a mean, red-faced child. "Everyone gets treated with respect in here—wives, husbands, therapists, everyone. So, no name-calling. Got it?"

Redmann was a powerful man, used to getting his way. But today was going to be different, and he knew it. Clearly he had no intention of getting help for his marriage or his wife. He came to disrupt so he could maintain his abusively neglectful control over her.

"My contract with Simon & Steele has nothing to do with why you're here today, as a matter of fact," I continued. "We can terminate my contract and get on with the business at hand." Though I meant those words, I was fairly certain he liked money too much to disturb our business dealings. I was right. He continued to pout, but his shoulders, as well as the lines in his face, seem to soften. He appeared to have backed down. I briefly glanced at Mrs. Steele, and then back at her bothered husband.

"Redmann, I know it wasn't easy for you to come here. I commend you for doing something most people won't and don't do. But I know you know that you're not just here for your wife. If this is too hard for you, I understand." Then I reached into my bag of techniques. "Redmann, you're free to leave. You're not a hostage here. This is hard work, and Ivy is good at hard work. Everyone's not cut out for this." I summarily turned to Mrs. Steele. "Ivy, when your husband leaves, we can continue on."

The mogul's eyes went from side to side in confusion. Savvy a businessman as Steele was, he easily succumbed to his immature, ego-driven sense of competition.

"Okay?" I asked him, placing the ball in his court.

"If I stayed, what would you want me to do?" Steele asked in a less abrasive tone.

"Just be a part of the process, not an observer. Tell me something about the two of you—perhaps your fondest memory of you and Ivy."

He tilted his head and furrowed his brow in question. Then he sighed, rolled his eyes, looked at his wife, and looked at me again. "*I'm* not doing this!" he barked. "I'm not your patient—*she* is. You coming, Ivy?" He got up and bolted toward the door. Ivy reached for her bag. Her big brown eyes glanced at me with regret and then embarrassingly drifted downward.

"Same time next week, Miss Ivy?" Kendall asked as the couple scurried past her desk.

"I'll call you," Ivy quickly spoke before closing the front door.

I stood in my office doorway, and watched them leave.

"Well, now, that was quick, Doc."

"Yes, it was, Kendall."

He's hiding something, I thought.

*   *   *   *

"Oh, my God, Slade we shouldn't be doing this! It's been so long," I uttered in ecstasy, as I had just taken a bite from a Bud's Broiler charbroiled hickory sauce burger. We were sitting in one of the shiny wooden booths of the old eatery. Feeling my friend's eyes on me, I stopped eating for a moment and looked up at him. "What?" I playfully asked.

"You have a—" He started to say, and then paused as he looked at my lips.

"A what?"

"A piece of bread on the side of your mouth." Slade then reached across the table and gently slid his finger along the side of my face to remove the morsel. *Oh, my,* I thought as my body reacted to his touch. *Back girl. He's got a girlfriend. Well, he started it!* I argued with myself.

"Did you get it?" I asked him.

"Yeah, Wintahs, I got it," Slade answered with a rascally grin.

"Commander Slade!" I emphasized his name in feigned incredulity, breaking the mood. My first thought was to tell Slade about seeing Aaron Quinn this morning, but I thought better. He was Mirandized, and I was pretty certain he had lawyered up.

So my visit to Aaron had to be on my own, void of the NOPD.

"When do you think the department's going take over the investigation?" I asked Slade. "Have they classified it as a murder yet?"

"Not yet. The Fire Department's holding on to it. Told ya, Wintahs, the lines run deep between us and them."

I stopped eating and looked at Slade, waiting to hear more, but he continued to stare. "What?" I finally said. "I know I don't have food on my face." I made sure by dabbing the sides of my mouth.

"I miss this."

"Miss what?" I asked him, though I was pretty certain I knew what he was talking about.

"This. Us. We make a good team."

We shared a prolonged gaze. *I miss you too,* I thought, but refused to say it out loud.

"Anyway, Wintahs, I know you saw the news."

"Yes, I did. So they found out where the bullet went that I heard that night."

"Yeah, so I think it's gonna be comin' our way soon. I'll see if I can't do some lobbyin' on this one for the two of us to handle it. It's pretty high-profile. I see you, Wintahs. What'cha got cookin' up there?"

I perked up at the chance to externally sift through the notes in my head. "Well, we know that there was an explosion. We know that there was a subsequent fire, we assume from the explosion. Right?"

"Right."

"We also know that three people died in that fire. And now we know that one of those three people was murdered. So let's assume that the fire was started on purpose."

"To cover up the murder."

"Right, to cover up the murder. That being the theory, there are basically five types of people that start fires."

"I'm listenin'."

I held up my forefinger. "The kid that just likes setting fires." I held up two fingers. "The guy that starts a fire so he can put it out, you know, so he can be the hero. And oftentimes, that guy's a fireman." I held up three fingers. "Then there's the guy that just likes doing it for self-gratification, the internal enjoyment of it."

"The pyromaniac," Slade said.

"Exactly!" I held up four fingers. "Then, there's the guy getting *paid* to set a fire."

"The sub-contractor," Slade sardonically jested.

I smiled at his unique way of redefining my description. "You could put it that way. He or she—usually a he, though—has no emotional attachment. He's just getting paid. And finally"—I held up all five fingers—"there's the revenge arsonist. For him, or her, it's personal. He or she sets the fire or pays someone to set the fire out of revenge, or anger, or fear of a secret being revealed."

Slade squared his elbows on the table and gave me a deadpan stare. "How and why do you know all of this seemingly useless information? You never cease to amaze me."

I chuckled at my friend's question. "A few years ago, I had a couple of patients that were pyromaniacs, and I had to research the behavior. Slade, there's just something in me. I can't know enough about how the human mind works. I love this stuff. It always brings me back to why I do what I do. I just want to know why people do what they do, good or bad. You know?"

Slade shook his head at my sense of commitment—or, rather, obsession.

"By the way," I continued, "speaking of people doing things, do you remember some time back when I had to call the police for an unwanted visitor at my home?"

"Yeah, I remember. The security guard from the Jefferson building. Jones, I believe, was his name. What about it?"

"Good memory, Slade. Calvin Jones, to be exact. Do you have any ideas where he might be these days?"

"Uhhh—nope. Why? What's up?"

"I think I saw him."

"You saw him. When, where?"

"Outside my office a few days ago, and yesterday at the lecture."

"Are you sure it was him?"

"Yeah, I think so. Both times he seemed to run, scatter when I looked his way. But I'm pretty certain it was him."

"What's his deal, Wintahs?"

"I don't know. I thought we'd put that to rest when he was detained for trespassing. Kind of sorry I didn't press charges."

"But back then you were pretty certain he was just a fanatic fan."

"Not anymore. My intuition tells me he's not just a fan."

"I'll see what I can come up with. In the meantime, I know I don't need to tell you this, but be careful, and the next time you see him, gimme a holla'. Don't you do anything."

I raised one eyebrow and twisted my mouth to the

side in playful defiance of my friend's suggestion.

"Whatever, Wintahs, about that fire, I'm leanin' towards Mr. Revenge."

"I'm with you on that one—wait a minute Slade. You hear that?" We both listened as Kool and the Gang's "Too Hot" filled the air from the jukebox. "I used to love that song.".

"Oh, yeah," Slade replied, as I picked a French fry off of his plate.

❧ CHAPTER 8 ❧

The line of people waiting to get into Willie Mae's Scotch House hung just outside the entrance. "How many people in ya party?" the oval-faced hostess asked as she looked me up and down.

"I'm actually meeting someone," I said. "Do you mind if I take a look around?"

"Help ya'self, dawlin.'"

I walked through the noisy eatery, inhaling the undeniably tempting aroma of fried chicken, their specialty. But my olfactory moment was halted by the site of my lunch date sitting off to the side of the re-furbished old restaurant.

"Well, hello, beautiful," Assistant D.A. Jay Childs said excitedly as he stood up, displaying his muscular frame through his tight navy-blue suit. He gave the length of my body a smooth raking-over and placed a soft kiss on my cheek.

He sure is nice to look at, I thought as I caught a whiff of his cologne through the redolence of smells in the air. "How are you, Jay?" I asked him, and then took a seat across from him.

"I'm doing well, Morgan. You're the one. How are you? Of course, if I were going by looks alone, I'd say you were doing great. You're looking as beautiful as ever."

"Well, now, don't you two make a pretty couple?" said a stout, rosy-mouthed waitress as she put two glasses of water onto our table. "My name is Minnie Faye, and I'm gonna be your server today." She handed each of us a menu. "Why don't y'all take a look at these menus, and I'll be back in a few minutes."

"Thank you, Minnie Faye," I responded, then turned to my date. "And thank you, Jay, for the complement. I'm doing well. But tell me, what's been going on with you?"

"As usual, I'm loaded down with cases these days, Morgan..." he began as I half-listened while thinking, *What a good-looking man. But where's the oomph I used to feel when we first met? It hasn't been that long. His youthful ways were a fun distraction from my busy life. But the excitement seems to be gone. Where's the spark?*

As I sat across from Jay and reassessed my physiological response to seeing him, I felt nothing other than fondness. *It's gone. What happened?* I wondered as a very dim light-bulb moment occurred in my head. *Damn you, Slade.*

I looked across the table and knew that today was probably the last lunch I would have with Jay Childs as half of a fledgling couple. My heart sank, just a little, at the disappointment of the revelation. With that, I turned the volume of my thoughts down, and Jay's words up.

"...and I tell you, Morgan, those guys are the worse at keeping things confidential. Do you know that Al Thomas, who works in ballistics with the NOPD, told me they believe the fire was set in order to cover up a murder?"

Jay usually had juicy tales, and a part of me enjoyed listening to and marinating on the spicy chinwags he would fill my ear with. The other part felt a tad guilty for taking part in gossip. But I perked right up and broke my fake moral gossip code when Jay digressed from his usual D.A. grapevine blather to the Quinn fire.

"Really? How'd he find that out?" I inquired.

"Y'all ready to order, ma' babies?" Minnie Faye broke in with pen and pad in hand.

Dang it! I privately uttered at the interruption. "Can we have a couple more minutes?"

"Sure, dawlin'." She looked at the line of people waiting to get in and then walked away.

"You were saying, Jay?"

"What was I saying?" He thought for a moment. "Oh, yeah, Al told me that his girlfriend told him." He paused to peruse the menu. "Yeah, there it is, the fried chicken," he decisively declared and put the menu down. "So, where was I? Oh, okay, so, like I said, he told me that his girlfriend told him. She happens to be one of the secretaries for the fire investigator's office."

"Do they have any evidence pointing to arson?"

"Not that I know of—but isn't that something! Even though you're not working on that case, I thought you might find that interesting. The things people leak never cease to amaze me. You ready to order?"

Jay signaled the waitress, not seeming to think twice about my added interest in his conversation. I wanted to press further, but I wasn't comfortable doing so. I was probably going to end the relationship today. So I changed the subject. "I love this place, Jay. It's been a while since I've been here."

"Yeah, me too."

Minnie Faye came over. "What y'all say, ma' babies? Y'all ready to order?"

"I think we are," Jay said. "I'll have the fried chicken, with a side of red beans and rice, and mustard greens. Oh, and add a sweet tea to that." He handed his menu back to the waitress.

"I don't know where you put it all," I told him, then turned to Minnie Faye. "I'll have the house salad and a diet Dr. Pepper."

"Okay, I'll put that order in, and I'll be right back with your drinks, all right?"

"Thank you," Jay and I told her in unison before she moved on.

"Enough about me, Morgan, and this side of the table. What about you? How's the recovery going since the accident? Who hit you, by the way? Did you really pull her out of the car right before it blew up?"

"The recovery's good. A lady by the name of Kassidy Kane hit me. And, yes, I did pull her out of her car before it blew up."

"Are you kidding me? You are something else, Morgan Winters. Don't let anybody tell you any different." Jay had a noticeable gleam of admiration in his eyes. I didn't feel comfortable putting off the inevitable any longer.

"Jay, I need to tell you something," I began.

"Okay, ma' babies, a sweet tea for you, and a Dr. Pepper for you." Minnie Faye placed our drinks on the table. "Be right back with your food."

Jay took a sip of his tea and licked his lips to the taste. "I'm all ears."

"It's about us."

"Us?"

"Okay, house salad for you." Our food appeared. "Fried chicken platter for you. I'm gonna leave y'all some extra napkins, ketchup and hot sauce. Y'all need anything else?"

"No, thank you," I told Minnie Faye. "Yes, us," I told Jay as he tilted his head to the side and leaned in closer. "Well..." I paused to see his now perceptively disappointed eyes suddenly looking back at me.

"You're kidding me," he said. "You're not about to say what I think you're going to say. Are you?

"Jay."

"Awww, man, what is this? I thought we were having fun."

"We were, Jay. It's just that."

"It's just that what?"

"It's just that I realized my heart's not where it should be, and I don't want to just have fun at the sake of your feelings."

"Y'all doin' okay?" Minnie Faye interrupted again, doing her job. "Y'all sure got quite over here. Can I get y'all somethin'?"

"Everything's just fine," Jay sardonically replied, smiling at the waitress. She believed him, though.

"Okay, ma' babies. Y'all call me if ya need any-thing."

"Think I'll be calling a cab," Jay mumbled.

"What's that, dawlin'?"

"Nothing, Minnie Faye, thank you," I told her.

Jay began to pick and pull at his food. "So that's it, huh, Morgan?"

"I'm afraid so, Jay. I don't want to lead you on."

"Not as hungry as I thought I was. Guess I'm done with this." He pushed the plate back, grabbed his nap-kin from his lap, wiped his mouth, and then placed it over the dish. He took fifty dollars out of his wallet and put it on the table. "That should cover it. Guess I'll see you around, Morgan." His dark eyes managed to momentarily penetrate mine, conveying his displea-sure, as he left the table and headed for the door.

"Crap!" I whispered to myself as I picked at my salad.

"Y'all need anything over here, dawlin'?" The wait-ress came back, looked at the empty chair and the money on the table, and gave me a sympathetic smile.

"No, thank you, Minnie Faye, just the check." My cellphone began to ring. "Yeah, Slade."

"Well, who stole your lunch money, Wintahs? What's goin' on over there? You don't sound so good."

"Yeah, not my best day. What'cha got?"

"Well, I got some news for ya."

"Give me some good news, Slade."

" 'Good news' is my middle name, Wintahs." My mood began to shift as I chuckled at Slade's quip. "That's what I'm talkin' 'bout. Here's the good news. We're on."

"We're on?"

"We're on, me and you. Superintendent Brison officially assigned the two of us to the Quinn case. Prelim autopsy report back, semi-public, and in the hands of the NOPD. It's officially a homicide. Ballistics report should be coming in soon. Got an interview set up this afternoon at six o'clock. You in?"

"Try to keep me out."

"Jus' what I thought you'd say. Mr. Donovan Quinn is first up. Like ol' times, Wintahs."

"Like ol' times, Slade."

*   *   *   *

"Well, you're back early, Doc," Kendall commented as she seemed to carefully watch me walk into the office. "And don't you have a pep to your step?" She frowned in curious delight.

"Yes, I am. And I guess I do." I winked at my secretary.

"Must be your lunch date with that handsome Mr. Childs." Kendall smiled and stacked some folders on her desk.

"Or not."

"Well, whatever it is, Doc, it looks good on you."

"Thank you, Kendall," I replied, just as the jazzy ringtone on my phone chimed.

"Yeah, Slade."

" Five-thirty instead of six still good?"

"Hold on a minute. Kendall, what time is my last patient for today?"

"Four."

"See you at five-thirty, partner."

"You know, Doc, I learned a thing or two from you."

"You did?"

"Uh-huh. Here's one of 'em. You always told me that a new mood equals a new thought, and a new thought means 'hot damn.' "

"I told you that?"

"Well, maybe not in those words, but, yeah, Doc, I learned that from you. And if you don't mind me saying. I think that the new mood on you comes from the new thought, that you must be workin' with Commanda' Slade on a case again. Am I right?" Kendall tilted her head, raised one eyebrow, and puckered her lips to the side in confident deduction.

"Lucky guess." I smirked at my secretary.

"I knew it! I knew it! The band's back together again. Reunited, and it feels so good, 'cuz he's still the one. Ain't he, Doc? Ain't he? You don't have ta' answer me. 'Cuz I know the answer."

I enjoyed Kendall's excitement, but then I noticed a piece of paper on her desk with Redmann's name on it. "What's this, Kendall?"

"Oh, Doc, Mr. Steele's office called and said that he wanted to meet with you at his downtown office Friday mornin'. Said it was very important. I checked your schedule. You're free that mornin'."

"Confirm it, then."

"Will do, Doc."

❧ CHAPTER 9 ❧

I walked by Slade's office and peered through the thin horizontal blinds. Slade was sitting at his desk talking to Donovan Quinn. I tapped on the door.

"It's open," Slade yelled out. "Dr. Quinn, I know you know Dr. Wintahs here."

The bestselling author, grieving husband and father stood up upon my entry. "Of course, Morgan, good to see you again. I was hopin' you would be in on this."

We shook hands. "Good to see you, too, Donovan. Please, sit." He retook his seat as I sat beside him. His broad shoulders slumped a bit, his elbows faced outward on the arms of his chair, and his hands rested on his thighs. He seemed relaxed. I mirrored his posture as much as I gracefully could to assuage the rapport.

"Wintahs, Dr. Quinn here just finished tellin' me what he remembers from the night of the fire. If you don't mind, Doctor, tell Dr. Wintahs what you just told me."

"Like I told Commander Slade, it all happened so quickly, Morgan," Quinn began as his dark, droopy eyes connected with mine. "I'd walked my last few guests to the curb. We'd been outside talking for a while."

"Who were your last few guests?"

Donovan looked up and to his left in recollection. "Redmann, Bill and Joan Conners."

"Anybody else?"

"Oh, yeah, I did see Dane's sister get into her car when I said goodnight to the Conners'."

"Anybody else?"

"No."

"What about your son, Aaron? Where was he?"

"Aaron was inside until the explosion. He came running out after all hell broke loose."

"When was the last time you remember seeing Dane?"

"It was very early on in the evening. Not sure what time it was. She was mingling with some guests. So much was going on."

"You don't remember seeing her at all during or after the toasts?"

"No, I don't." Quinn looked off in frozen thought.

Neither did I, I thought. *In fact, I didn't see Dane Quinn at all that night.* Donovan seemed relaxed, but he was robotically recanting that night. *He's not relaxed. For whatever reason, his affect is scaled back, his movements are a little slower than I remember. He might be medicated. I'm going to try to reboot this.*

"Donovan," I said as I touched his hand to break his trend of thought, "I'm going to fix myself a cup of coffee. Can I get you a fresh cup or some water?"

"Uhh—yeah," he replied. "I'll have a fresh cup. Thanks."

I got up and eyed Slade, letting him know that it was time to switch things up.

"Tell ya what," he said. "I'm gonna let the two of you talk for a minute. I need to organize some notes here. So, if y'all don't mind, I'm gonna sit right back here."

He moved behind Quinn and me to his old beat-up brown leather couch. It sat off to the side, under his office window. Somehow, that corner of Slade's office concealed itself from the light in the room. You could easily forget someone was sitting back there.

"I see you're going to be doing a book-signing tomorrow, Donovan," I told him while I fixed two cups of coffee. "You've been going nonstop. I bet you could use a break."

"Yeah, I could, Morgan, but since all of this the sales have been through the roof. I'm in more demand than ever. Redmann tells me, and I agree, it's good to be busy, and sales are usually good when you're busy. So I've been on auto-pilot since the fire. I think I'm afraid to stop. By the way, I'm giving a lecture next week as part of my *Fix Your Life* series. I'd be honored if you could attend as one of my guests."

"Absolutely. All I need to do is check my calendar, Donovan. Cream and sugar?"

"Yeah, that's fine."

"It's hot." I handed him the beverage and took my seat. His posture remained open, but the remoteness in his eyes continued to tell a different story. "I have to ask you, Donovan—what would a break look like for you these days?"

"Honestly, I don't know. When I allow my mind to wander, the pain cuts too deep to stay there long. I'm not ready." Quinn released eye contact from me and stared off and away again.

"How's Aaron?"

"Not good, but at least he's alive. I go to see him every chance I get. He's still not happy to see me, but at least he's not trying to kill me, or himself, these days. That might be up for debate, though, huh? He is tied down, after all."

Quinn half-smiled and then took a sip of coffee. The room went quiet again.

"Donovan, talk to me about Donnie Jr. and Ashleigh."

"What do you want to know?" He sat up taller and folded his arms, appearing no longer as relaxed. A tinge of anger suddenly flashed in his eyes. His guard was down enough for at least anger to seep out, I decided to lean in and dig deeper.

"Did you hear one of them laugh? Did they hug you before they said goodbye that night?"

Quinn's wall of defenses began to crack as he battled to maintain his comportment. He pursed his lips and clinched his fists. Then his square jaw tightened in a futile attempt to maintain his external calm. His face contorted in hurt-filled agony as his eyes watered.

Bingo. That's the way into his heart.

I made eye contact with Slade in recognition of Quinn's pain. Slade lifted his hands, asking me whether or not I wanted him to come back over. I shook my head.

"They were beautiful," Quinn said tearfully. "They were so beautiful. They were the joy of my life. The last time I saw them, earlier that night, Donnie Jr. was wearing his favorite shirt, a Captain America shirt. And Ashleigh was looking like daddy's little girl. Every time I close my eyes, I see them. I see them when my eyes are open. I don't know how to deal with this. They weren't supposed to be there. Daddy's so sorry. I'm so sorry." His pain poured out as he wept.

"No need to apologize, Donovan."

We sat for a moment as he dealt with his pain.

"Where were they supposed to be?" I tiptoed back into the conversation.

"Huh?"

"Ashleigh and Donnie Jr. You said they weren't supposed to be there. Where were they supposed to be?"

"Their Aunt Kassie was supposed to pick them up and bring them to a friend's house for the night, but she didn't."

"Aunt Kassie is Dane's sister, your sister-in-law, right?"

"Yes. I haven't been able to bring myself to even look at her since that night. If she'd only done what she was supposed to do, they would still be alive. Anyway, you know the rest." The author sniffed a couple of times and vigorously wiped his face clean with a handkerchief.

"Do you know why she didn't take the kids that night, Donovan?"

"No, I just assumed she'd made some sort of arrangement with Dane. I didn't know. How was I supposed to know? You saw me that night, Morgan. I had so much going on. The next thing I know, they're bringing my dead children out of the house. I didn't even know they were there."

"I can't imagine, Donovan. I can't even imagine."

Quinn rubbed his forehead in what appeared to be perplexed sadness. I glanced at Slade, signaling that I was just about done.

"All right, there, Dr. Quinn," Slade told him. "Thank you for comin' down here at the last minute, and we'll call ya if anything comes up. Oh, one more thing. This is a standard question, but what kind of insurance policy did you have on your family, if any?"

Quinn's face turned ever so slightly in controlled upset. He was guarded again. The tears were gone. "We had a standard policy, Commander. I'm not sure exactly how much. What are you getting at?"

"Nothing, Doctor, absolutely nothing. It's a standard question. We just have to check all the boxes. I'm pretty certain the Fire Department asked you the same thing, right?"

"They did."

"See, it's standard. So can you get back with me on that one?"

Quinn shook his head, agreeing to Slade's request.

"Wait, Donovan," I interjected. "I just want to remind you of something. I'm here to help figure out who took your family from you. I'm also here as a therapist, so any time you want to talk, you have my number."

"Thank you so much, Morgan. I think I'm going to take you up on that, when I get some time."

Slade held the door open as Quinn walked out of the office, and then closed the door. We both looked through the blinds until we couldn't see him anymore.

"What'd'ya make of that?"

"Slade, that man is in pain. He fit the textbook description of someone in pain. But every now and then, when he talked, his eyes would drift. Could just be his way of dealing with so much loss. I don't know him that well. I do know, though, that he's a cool customer."

"Oh, yeah, Wintahs, they don't come much smoother. But he ain't nickel-slick. He's polished. Tough nut to crack, huh?"

"Yeah, I don't know. He is definitely hard to read. But his emotion was real, especially when he talked about his kids. Not so much when he talked about his wife, though."

"Yeah, the one with the bullet in her skull."

"Right. Doesn't mean he killed anybody, though. At this point, it just means that we have to dig—"

"Deeper."

"Finishing my sentences, huh, Commander?"

"What can I say? I know ya, Wintahs."

"That you do. Unlike Quinn, with him we'll have to let the facts reveal themselves. Since we really don't know him, he could most definitely be hiding something, anything."

"Anything. Yeah, he did have a bit of a reaction when we brought up insurance."

"He did. But, you know, we all have secrets."

"Got that right, Wintahs. Oh, by the way, got something for ya."

"For me?"

"Just for you." Slade reached into one of his desk drawers, pulled out a big stack of files labeled 'QUINN HOMICIDE,' and handed it to me. "Merry Christmas."

❧ CHAPTER 10 ❧

Generally speaking, the only office I didn't mind going to downtown was mine. Otherwise, during the day, the CBD—also known as the city business district of New Orleans—was full of red lights, traffic, expensive parking, and tunnel-visioned drivers. I had grown tolerant of going to my publishers, but even that had grown into a chore.

Simon & Steele's offices were on St. Charles Avenue, occupying the top three floors of the Place St. Charles building. After my last encounter with Steele in my office, I had begun to wonder how much longer we would be working together. This visit was more of a challenge than usual.

"Great!" I said out loud as I found a parking space a block down from the building at a meter. That was the best thing about driving the small rental I was given: I could fit in the tightest of spaces. I backed the little car into the spot, took a quick look in the mirror, added some lipstick, put my shoes on, dropped some change in the meter, and headed up the street.

A large corporate white receptionist desk greeted me as I stepped out of the elevator and into the posh office space of Simon & Steele. It was sleek, modern, and over-the-top high-end. Beyond the receptionist area stood wall after wall of glass-partitioned offices. Once I was actually in, the flashy modern décor took over. It was so plush that it was enjoyable to look at. Steele's corner workspace was massive—full of the pomp and bigness of his personality.

"Good morning, Dr. Winters," said the young receptionist at the desk. "Mr. Steele is expecting you. Please have a seat. He'll be with you in a minute."

Hmmm. This was a departure from the other times I had visited Steele's office, when he had practically met me at the elevator. I wondered if this had anything to do with the last time we had seen each other. *Of course it does, Morgan.*

After ten minutes though in the plush reception area, my patience for Steele's antics—if that's what they were—were beginning to grow short. "Excuse me, is he going to be much longer?" I asked the receptionist.

"I'm not certain, ma'am."

"Well, can you check on that for me?"

"Yes, ma'am." Just then, though, the receptionists' phone rang. "Yes, sir." She hung up and turned to me. "Mr. Steele is ready to see you now. His secretary, Chessa, will escort you to his office. There she is, now."

A tall, Nordic-looking blond emerged from the corridor of offices. "Pleasure to see you again, Dr. Winters," she said. "Right this way."

I gathered my belongings, and we were off, down the long hallway. Steele's office sat at the end of the corridor. Chessa opened the curved frosted double doors to Steele's office, where he sat behind his desk on the phone.

"Yes, that's right, Michael." He gestured for me to take a seat in one of the white leather chairs in front of his long, steel-bottomed, glass-topped desk. Then he swiveled his chair away from me. Again, this meeting was quite different from the other times I had come in to see him. If I had any doubt, it was clear at this point that his inattentive, borderline rude actions were intentional.

Intentional or not, this is unacceptable, I thought. "Redmann, I'm leaving," I told him as I stood up. "You know where to find me."

"Hold on, Michael." He turned to me. "Don't leave, Morgan. I'm almost done." He turned back to his phone. "Okay, you let them know, and we'll talk later." He finally hung up his 'very important' call and turned his full attention toward me. "Morgan, I'm so glad you were able to come by," he told me with no apology.

"Absolutely, Redmann. What's this all about?" I was now clearly on the defense.

"I just thought that we needed to clear up a few things. Would you like some coffee, tea, or some water?"

"No, thank you. I'm fine."

"Nonsense, Chessa, could you bring a bottle of VOSS for the Doctor?" he spoke through his intercom.

"Yes, sir, Mr. Steele, right away," I heard his secretary say. Soon thereafter, a soft rap on the door made itself known. Then Chessa entered, holding a silver tray with a glass and a frosted bottle of VOSS water. "For you, Dr. Winters."

"Thank you." I took the glass and the bottle. Now, what's going on, Redmann? Kendall told me that you called with some degree of urgency."

"Will that be all, Mr. Steele?"

"Until I want something else. Thank you, Chessa. Shut the door behind you."

"Yes, Mr. Steele."

Chessa closed the door and Steele turned toward me, appearing finally ready to get down to business. "I just thought that we needed to clear up a few things, Morgan?"

"Clear up a few things? If this is about the new

contract, Redmann, if it's okay with you, my lawyers need a little more time, to make sure everything is in order."

"Oh, no, no, take all the time you need. This isn't about the contract, and I don't mean to sound so cryptic."

The hell you don't. I thought as I crossed my legs and folded my arms in defense of a possible passive-aggressive preemptive strike from my publisher. *Something tells me this is not going to be fun.*

"It's just that after the other day I really felt the need for this conversation."

And there it is. This has nothing to do with business. This is about him settling the score, for a perceived slight, from the other day.

"Is that so?" I retorted. "What about the other day?"

Steele looked around his office, especially the front door, as if to make sure we were alone. He sat on the front of his desk, up and over me. His face went suddenly hard and cold. "We'll talk about that in a minute. First, I was going through your numbers, and I'm not liking what I'm seeing."

"What you're *seeing?* My numbers, my sales, have been above average and steady, Redmann. What are you talking about?"

"Well, yes and no. It's just that they're not up to

par with some of our other authors, and we're starting to doubt your abilities along those lines."

"Is that so?"

"Yeah, nothing personal, Morgan." Steele smiled and then sat behind his desk. "So we're just going to scale back on your marketing, and reclassify you and your project as developmental."

My face frowned and twisted at his passive assault. "So, let me get this right. You're telling me that you are suddenly concerned that I'm not going to be able to maintain the exceptional sales numbers that I've been holding for the last year. Therefore, you're going to scale back the marketing for my book and reclassify how you proceed?"

"Well, you see, now, you're taking this the wrong way, Morgan."

"The hell I am!" I felt my blood pressure rise as he leaned back in his big leather chair and gave me a feigned sympathetic smile. He sadistically enjoyed my dismay, feeding off my anger, reveling in my defensiveness.

"Let me tell you something, Morgan. You might have had your way the other day in your office, but you're in *my* office now, and if you want to keep on writing books for Simon & Steele Publishing, you better recognize who's running this show. I'm the best publisher around, and you're lucky to be here. Simon & Steele is getting ready to take over the world. This is the biggest company you can ever hope to be a part of. I'm in control in here, okay?"

His nostrils flared in fury as he starred me down. In that moment I released myself from this unhealthy interaction. Forget right or wrong, good or bad—his fears, his self-perceived inadequacies, and his ability to live in perpetual denial governed his actions. I could see that no amount of diplomacy, or anger on my part, was going to right this course. This was *his* issue. This interaction made it crystal clear to me that I, under no circumstances, wanted to work with this very emotionally unhealthy man.

"You know what, Redmann? Your willingness to forgo sound business practices for this contrived drama…"

"Contrived drama?!? You're a second-rate…"

Right then I stood up and made piercing eye contact with Steele and his belligerent, abusive tone. Just like a bully, he got quiet and backed down.

"Yes, contrived, manufactured drama," I asserted, "meant to exact some surreptitious hostile revenge on me for maintaining order in my office. I mistakenly thought that your business acumen was your driving force. Clearly I was wrong. Power and wealth look good on you, Redmann. The childlike insecurity, not so much. As you've aptly pointed out to me, you're not my patient, and I don't need this headache. Simon & Steele will no longer be connected to my future earnings potential. When the current contract is up, we're done. Any questions, talk to my attorneys. Oh, and by the way, there's good help out there. Get some. You don't have to be this way."

I picked my bag up and walked out in lucid serenity.

"Goodbye, Dr. Winters," Chessa told me as I walked past her.

"Have a great day, Chessa. Mine just got considerably better."

*   *   *   *

"'Mornin', Doc," Kendall greeted me as soon as I stepped into my office. Her eyes, bright and wide more often than not, were unusually so today. In a rather awkward manner, she darted them back and forward toward the waiting room. This was her attempt to draw my attention to Ivy Carlisle Steele's presence in one of the chairs.

"Good morning, Kendall."

"'Morning, Ivy. Surprised to see you here today. Did we have an appointment?"

"Forgive me, Doctor. I thought it very important to see you as soon as possible. If I could just have a word with you, I would appreciate it."

I lingered my gaze on her after she spoke. Behind her well-put-together veneer was an urgent look of desperation in her eyes. I turned to Kendall.

"Your first patient is due at nine-fifteen, Doc."

"Come on in, Ivy. I have some time before my first patient. Kendall, hold my calls."

"Okay, Doc."

"Have a seat," I told Ivy as she sauntered by in a *prêt-à-porter* yellow pants suit. As usual, the outside in no way told what was going on inside. I placed my keys and bag on my desk as we both took a seat. "So tell me, Ivy. What's going on?"

She looked down and then took a deep breath. "First, Doctor, I'd like to apologize for the last session. We had no right to come in here like that. Funny, here I am apologizing for an unexpected visit, and, surprise, here I am again." She lightly chuckled.

I smiled back at her. "I'm pretty certain you didn't come down here this morning to apologize for what you perceived to be an inconvenience. Tell me, Ivy, why are you here this morning?" My brow slightly furrowed with concern as I noticed how she floundered in discomfort. Her foot danced behind her double-crossed legs. Her hands were so tightly clasped that her knuckles were white. "What's going on, Ivy? You're safe here. Tell me. What's going on?"

We sat in silence until she finally took a deep breath and began to speak.

"You're right, Doctor, I didn't come here to apologize. I came here to tell you something about my husband." Ivy nervously looked around the room, as if to make sure no one else was listening. "Redmann talks in his sleep. When we first married, I would listen and try to understand what he was saying. As time went on, I became bored with the occurrence, and learned to sleep through it. But a few nights ago, that changed."

"What happened?"

"His sleep-talking started off as it always did, with loud mumbling waking me up. But that time, as I attempted to go back to sleep, the mumbling grew more and more agitated, louder, and clearer."

"Clearer?"

"Yes, clearer. Instead of nonsensical utterings, this time in no uncertain words, I heard him say, 'I'm going to kill you, Dane,' over and over again, each time with more and more venom, until I shook him awake."

"What happened after you woke him up?"

"He went back to sleep, and I laid awake the rest of the night. I didn't know what to do, until I finally told myself today that I should say something. I've been carrying this secret around as if I'd done something wrong." Ivy sat back in unburdened relief.

Humph, I thought, pondering therapist-patient confidentiality, and whether or not I would be in breach of it by talking to Slade about what I had just heard. *He's not my patient.* I reflected back to Steele point-blank telling me so, but my better professional half told me to say something to my client: "Ivy, I need to tell you, there are limits to our confidentiality with what you've just told me. I am officially working with the NOPD on the Quinn murder investigation now, and this might come into play. In fact, it will."

"I assumed that it would, Doctor. I have no qualms with that."

"Okay, then." *9:05, darn it!* I thought as I looked at the clock hanging above Ivy's head. *Not much time left before my first client.* There was so much more I wanted to ask, but instead I used the allotted time to inquire about her safety and her husband's whereabouts. "Where's Redmann now?"

"He's off to D.C. for business."

"For how long?"

"I'm always uncertain of these things, Doctor, but this time he did say this was an unexpected trip and he wouldn't be gone long. I do believe he enjoys my being out of sync with his comings and goings. So 'how long' is quite relative to Redmann. Do what you must with the information I've just given you. As long as he doesn't know that it came from me."

"You did the right thing by coming in here today, Ivy, and I'm afraid my patient is here," I said as I noticed the red light flashing on the intercom system.

"In the meantime, I have to ask you, do you feel safe at home?"

"Oddly enough, Doctor, I do. I don't think my husband is a killer. But since it was revealed that Dane Quinn was murdered, I haven't been able to stop thinking about what I heard. Hence, my visit to see you. Truth be told, he didn't say he wanted to kill *me*. And I think you know me well enough to know that, no matter what, I'm a survivor."

That you are, I thought. "Ivy, I'm going to ask you to give me a call as soon as you know he's back in town. Here's my personal cell number." I wrote my number on the back of one of my business cards and handed it to her. "Keep this with you."

"I will. I suppose I should be going now. Thank you again for seeing me on such short notice. I know I've given you an earful. But I figured who better to have as a therapist when something like this occurs. Right?"

"I couldn't agree with you more, Ivy."

❧ CHAPTER 11 ❧

"Come on, Slade," I said, after three rings. I was multi-tasking, holding the phone between my shoulder and my ear while I brushed my teeth. It had been a long day, and I was looking forward to crashing, but not before talking to Slade about Steele.

"Wintahs!"

"Slade! I was just planning my message for your voicemail."

"No need for that. What'cha got?"

Something in me wanted to smile and unwind upon hearing his raspy voice, but instead I went straight to the facts: "So, when did you say you were going to talk to Steele?"

"I didn't."

"Well, can we put him on the list?"

"Uhhh—yeah, I guess. What's up, Wintahs? What'cha know?"

"How about, a source told me that one Redmann Steele was overheard threatening Dane Quinn's life?"

"Oh, yeah, I can work with that. That's a good one. How soon you wanna see him? Wait a minute—what about the publishing stuff?"

"What about it?" I sternly asked.

"Ahh, that's your publishing company, right?"

"Not any more, Slade."

"Whoa. When did that happen?"

"Today."

"That's it?"

"In a nutshell, he called me into his office in an attempt to put me in my place and let me know who was in control."

"I take it that didn't go so well."

"No, it didn't. The conversation was short and to the point. Once I saw where he was going, I shut it down for good."

"What about your book deals?"

"I can get another book deal, or not, Slade. Either

way, I'm good."

"I believe that. What about the interview? How's that gonna work?"

"I don't think that's going to be a problem. I've dealt with people like Steele before."

"I believe that, too. So how 'bout I get him in here ASAP?"

"Well, he's out of town right now."

"Where is he? You know what? Doesn't matter. No need in spookin' him with a phone call, wherever he is. I'll just wait 'til he's back. But we're gonna need to know when he's back. Your source?"

"You got it, my source. The plan is for me to get a call as soon as he's back in town."

"Done."

"On that same note, Slade, guess who agreed to see me tomorrow?"

"Tomorrow, Saturday? Ahhh, you got me, Win-tahs, who?"

"Ms. Kassidy Kane."

"Speed Racer?"

"Yes, also known as Kassidy Kane."

"Okay, I see that. She's family. She might be able to

fill in a few missing pieces."

"Well, she's got a little more heads-up on her than that."

"What'cha know?"

"Well, I went to see Aaron Quinn the day after he pulled that gun at UNO."

"You went down to the rich boy's prison."

"Yes, I went to St. Paul's, asked to see him, and they let me in. You know why I didn't tell you—"

"Yeah, I know, he was Mirandized and lawyered up. He wasn't talkin' to us, and we couldn't talk to him. But you could."

"Exactly."

"What'd ya get?"

"Not much that we didn't already know. But he did tell me that I might want to talk to his Aunt, Kassidy. So I'm talking to his Aunt Kassidy tomorrow."

"Good deal. After all, there's some unaccounted for time on her end, and let's not forget that she was hammered that night."

"Right." I yawned.

"What else you got going over there?" Slade asked as I pulled my covers back, slid between the sheets, and flipped the TV onto QVC.

"Ahhhhh," I moaned in ecstasy at the comfort of my bed.

"Hold on there, Wintahs. This ain't that kinda' call."

I snickered at his suggestion, but thought I would give him one back for a change. "Oh, but it is. What are you wearing?" I told him in my most seductive voice.

His silence was louder than any word I had ever heard him say. I sat for a minute and pretended to wait for an answer. He was rarely at a loss for words, but tonight he was.

"Oh, I'm just kidding, Slade," I finally told him. "I'm in for the night. I just got in bed and flipped the TV on. Been a long week, you know, that thing at UNO, that old man, breaking up with Jay."

"Breaking up with Jay?"

"Oh, crap. Did I say that out loud?"

"Yes, you did."

"Anyway, after I talk to Miss Kane tomorrow, I plan on relaxing for the rest of the day. Of course, that will include thumbing through a chart or two, but Morgan's going to actually take the day off, kind of. And, yes, I broke up with Jay. What about you, Slade? What's your weekend look like?"

"Wait a minute. Wait a minute. Not so fast. So you're not seeing Mr. Pretty Boy anymore?"

"His name is Jay, and no, I'm not. So what about you? What's your weekend look like?" I attempted to move on again.

"Well, funny you should ask, Wintahs."

I braced myself for the possibility of hearing about his plans with his new girlfriend.

"I was just telling myself the other day that I was gonna do the *carpe diem* thing."

"The *carpe diem* thing?"

"Yeah, Wintahs, you know, *carpe diem.* 'Seize the day.' "

"Yeah, yeah, Slade, I know what *carpe diem* means. But what does it mean to you, and what day are you trying to seize?"

"I'm glad you asked. I'd like to seize tomorrow around seven p.m. with you."

He got me. I was the speechless one now.

"Hello, Wintahs, you there?"

"Yeah, I'm here, Slade."

"Okay, jus' didn't hear anything."

"Ahh—aren't you dating someone?"

"Not anymore. Well, the truth is, Wintahs, Lo and me were really just friends. We went out a couple of times, but the spark just wasn't there. She always seemed a bit preoccupied."

"Is that right?"

"Yep! So, pick you up tomorrow for seven?" I contemplated the thought with an internal smile.

"See you tomorrow for seven, Slade."

*   *   *   *

"You have arrived at 707 Opelousas, on your left," the robotic voice of my GPS told me as I pulled up in front of the home of Ms. Kassidy Kane. It was a typical New Orleans neighborhood. The street was lined with shotgun homes on both sides—rectangular-shaped wooden structures perched on concrete blocks. They all sat a couple of feet off the ground, each with its own flavor. It was actually only a few blocks from the Quinn home. Ms. Kane's place had a camelback rising in the rear, setting it apart from the rest. It sat behind a waist-high front-lawn fence.

As I scanned the neighborhood, I noticed a rapturous pecan tree providing shade for four gray-haired old men playing checkers on the neutral ground. *That's neighborhood watch,* I deduced as I propped my aviator sunglasses on my forehead and took a quick look at myself in the rearview mirror. I wiped the excess lipstick from the sides of my mouth, pulled my shades back over my eyes; slid back into my Louboutins, and got out of the car.

"Morning, fellas." I waved at the group of men.

"How you doing, pretty lady?" I could feel them following me with their eyes.

"I'm doing. How y'all?"

"Doin' a lot bettah since you pulled up."

I cordially nodded and smiled as I continued to walk toward Ms. Kane's house. The waist-high front gate was open, so I walked through. The concrete walkway, stairs and porch were uneven, chipped and worn with character.

The front door was guarded by an old gray screen that squeaked and leaned slightly to the side when opened. I swung back the screen and rapped on the door. 'Clank, clank, clank' went the black Mardi Gras mask-shaped door-knocker. No one answered. 'Clank, clank, clank,' I tapped again. Still no answer. *Hm-mmmm.*

I closed the screen door and slowly paced the length of the porch, looking around for any signs of life. *People really should invest in blinds*, I thought as I peeped into one of Ms. Kane's blind-less windows, zeroing in on the room's contents. *Oh, my, a place for everything, and everything in its place.* The room was monochromatic white, with splashes of blood-red pillows on the two white sofas. The only other thing of a different hue in the room was a large bold crucifix on the wall. *She let God into her home. Good to know.*

"She's home! Keep knockin'!" yelled one of the men sitting outside, startling me out of my peeping Tom-like behavior and away from Ms. Kane's window. Embarrassed, I awkwardly waved and nodded at them in acknowledgment of their unsolicited advice. I walked back to the front door, opened the screen and knocked again, this time with a little more force, still to no answer. "What the...?" A black cat suddenly appeared out of nowhere at my feet, purring and rubbing against my leg. I let the screen door close as the affectionate feline demanded my attention.

"Dr. Winters?" went a soft, plain voice that seemed to come from a distance.

"Ahh, yes," I responded in wide-eyed alertness to the silhouetted figure that had just appeared from behind the screen door. "Ms. Kane?"

"Yes, come in." She held the door open as she revealed her entire frame. I flashed back to the lady in red at the party and the lady on the CCC, who were quite different from the person before me. She wore her hair down and free, as if she had just washed it, and was letting it dry naturally. Her charcoal-gray sweats and sneakers normalized her appearance. But she was still quite beautiful. "I see you've met Delilah." The cat purred, seemingly at the mention of her name, and then jumped into Ms. Kane's arms.

"Yes, we've met." I quickly scanned the room, seeing no dust or dirt, nothing out of place.

"Have a seat, Doctor. Please excuse the mess. I haven't been able to have the place cleaned since the accident and all." I looked around again for a speck of dust or anything out of order. Couldn't find it. The place was obsessively clean.

"Your home is beautiful, Ms. Kane. Is that a hand-knotted India Piazza rug on the floor?"

"Yes, it is."

"It's beautiful."

"Thank you, Doctor. It was a gift. Oh, and can I take this opportunity to say thank you for what you did on the bridge? I can never repay you. You saved my life."

"You're welcome. Anybody would have done the same."

"I beg to differ, Doctor. You risked your life to save mine, and I'm eternally grateful."

"Speaking of that night, how are you doing? You were banged up pretty bad."

"Yes, I was, I think I'm okay, though. Still very sore. I would love to get back to work as soon as possible."

"Very good. What do you do, Ms. Kane, if you don't mind my asking?"

"I don't mind at all. I'm an administrative assistant for Quinn Enterprises."

"As in Donovan Quinn?"

"Yes. I'm Donovan's secretary."

"I didn't know that. So we've spoken before?" I took a seat on one of her contemporary white sofas.

"Yes, but not that often."

"Oh, and I don't want another minute to go by without telling you how sorry I am for your loss."

She just looked at me.

"Your sister, your niece and nephew. I can't imagine what you must be feeling."

Ms. Kane gave me a placid, bland smile. "Care for some tea?"

"Oh, ahh—yes." I went along with her digression. *Okay, people respond to different things in different ways,* I reassured myself. *We just met. She doesn't have to be in a flood of tears at the mention of the tragedy.*

"I'll be back in a minute."

Off she went through the open area leading to the next room. I strained my neck to look beyond the passageway, but I couldn't see a thing. It was unusually dark beyond the room we were in. I quickly grabbed the black-rimmed specs out of my bag and walked over to get a closer look at the cross. The sculpture of Christ was intricately exquisite, depicting his death and pain with delicate beauty. The walnut post, the crosspiece, and the INRI nameplate appeared to be of solid gold. It was clearly of the finest quality.

"Sugar?" Ms. Kane suddenly re-entered the room from the shadowed area of the house with a formal tea setting on a tray.

"None for me, thank you."

"So, what's this all about? How can I help you, Doctor?"

"Well, I wanted to talk to you about the night of the fire."

"Okay, what would you like to know?"

"Well, what do you remember about that night, Ms. Kane?"

The delicate sound of metal against porcelain filled the room as she slowly stirred her tea. With no eye contact, she took a sip from the cup, placed it on the tray, and wiped the sides of her mouth with one of the white cloth napkins. I sat in the uncomfortable quiet and waited for an answer. I got the sense that Ms. Kassidy Kane was used to this kind of interaction. Her controlling nature was on full display.

After an extensive amount of time spent mixing her tea, she placed her spoon on the tray and looked into my eyes. Her face turned bold and hardened. "I honestly don't remember much."

"I see. Well, Ms. Kane, can you tell me about your relationship with your sister, then?"

"We weren't very close. Not much to tell."

"Okay, I understand." *More than you know,* I said to myself. "Thank you so much for your time. Before I leave, though, do you mind if I use your bathroom?"

"Certainly. Pass the first room and to your right." She gestured toward the dark passageway. I grabbed my oversized bag and made my way toward the area.

Since I wasn't able to get much of anything from Ms. Kane just yet, an unauthorized self-guided tour of her home would have to suffice. The sound of my shoes on the old hardwood floors echoed through the small shotgun house. The first room to my right was bare except for a chair, a lamp, a table, a bottle of pills, a glass of water, and an open Bible. In the corner sat an old wooden padded prayer-kneeler. I looked longingly at the light-switch but dared not flip it on. So I pulled my cellphone out and tiptoed into the empty room. I slowly picked up the bottle of pills and flashed the light from my phone onto it. 'Zolpidem,' it read. *Hmmm—she's having trouble sleeping, not surprising.* The old Bible was open to a particular section that was highlighted and underlined—one of the few verses I knew: *We know that our old self was crucified with Him in order that the body of sin might be brought to nothing, so that we would no longer be enslaved to sin. For one who has died has been set free from sin.*

I scanned the rest of the room. Nothing else was there. "Humph," I said quietly.

"You find everything okay?" Ms. Kane's voice yelled from the front room.

"Oh, yes." I scurried to the bathroom, washed my hands, and quickly made my way back toward the front room. "Well, I thank you so much for your time, Ms. Kane."

"Oh, are we done, Doctor.?" She seemed to be in genuine surprise.

"Pretty much. One thing, though, before I go, if you don't mind."

"Yes?"

"I couldn't help but notice your prayer room."

Kassidy's eyes quickly focused onto mine.

"The scripture your Bible was open to, Romans 6:6-7, can be very freeing. Can't it?"

Just then, Delilah reappeared at my feet as I began to make my way toward the front door. I took out a business card and handed it to Ms. Kane. "Here's my card. If you remember anything, or if you just want to talk, call me."

❧ CHAPTER 12 ❧

"Quiet, Maslow, quiet!" Only one person elicited that kind of excitement from my dog. "Coming!" I yelled as I stopped to take one last look in my foyer mirror. I blotted some of the red from my full lips, adjusted the black form-fitting mini I was wearing, and fluffed my hair.

What if this doesn't work, and I lose my friend? What if he finds out he doesn't like me that way, and I lose my friend? What if I don't like him that way, and I lose my friend? Well, how about this? What if I really like him, that way, and he really likes me, that way, and it's all good?

Now breathe. Let's live in the moment, not the 'what if.'

I took another deep breath, and I opened the door.

There he was, looking larger than life, as he blocked what was left of the setting sun. Before I could say a word, a soft, warm breeze ushered in the scent of his cologne, Gray Flannel. *I love it. He's so old-school.*

"Lookin' good, Wintahs.'" Slade smiled as his eyes gently raked my body over from head to toe.

"Why, thank you, Commander. Not lookin' too shabby yourself. Come in for a minute." Returning the favor, I gave him a full body scan as he walked by. *Very nice*, I thought as the brown hound's-tooth blazer and crisp white shirt, brought a glow to his olive complexion. He looked good, very good.

"Oh, these are for you." He revealed a bouquet of pink roses from behind his back.

"Why, thank you again, Commander Slade. They're beautiful." My eyes and heart lit up at the sight of the thoughtful gift.

"Blue-light special, $5.99," Slade told me as he gave me his most deadpan stare and nod. I pursed my lips into a skeptical smile. "What? You don't believe me? Bet you *he* believes me!"

"Arf! Arf!" Maslow barked after patiently waiting his turn.

"Hey there, boy. Who's a fibber? I'm not a fibber. How ya doin' boy? I miss you too!" *Those two have always had a thing.* While they frolicked like long lost friends, I slid my black YSL red-bottomed pumps on and grabbed my purse.

"I'm ready."

"Well, let's roll, then."

*   *   *   *

"Table pour deux?" the maître d' asked us as we walked into one of the quaintest French restaurants, in the city, Café Degas.

"Deux," Slade told the petite hostess as he held up two fingers.

"Serez-vous manger à l'intérieur, ou à l'extérieur?

"L'extérieur," Slade answered the lady again in her native tongue, pointing to the alfresco area of the restaurant.

"Par ici." The maître d' began to walk.

"After you, Wintahs." We followed the young lady to beautiful amber string-lit outdoor seating.

"Madame, monsieur. Votre serveur pour ce soir est François. Il sera bientôt avec vous. D'accord?"

"Oui, merci," Slade responded to the hostess one last time, and she showed us to our seats.

"Je suis tellement impressionnée. Je n'avais aucune idée que vous parlez français, Slade," I told him in

French how impressed I was with his language skills, and that I had no idea he spoke French.

"Whoa, whoa, Wintahs. I know enough high-school French to get us to our table. But that's where it stops."

I brought my hand up to my mouth to stifle my laugh as we both chuckled at his honesty. "I'm still impressed Slade. I love it!" I told him as the light from the candle on the table brought out the manly shadow of his beard.

"You like?" Slade asked as one of the busboys filled our glasses with water.

"I like. I like a lot."

*   *   *   *

"So, you're tellin' me, Wintahs, that Speed Racer didn't spill anything?" Slade asked me as I tasted a bit of the hanger steak I had ordered.

"As Kendall would say, nada, zilch, zippo, no-thing. She and I sat in the front room of her house for I'd say no longer than ten minutes or so. Everything in that room was white."

"What do you mean?"

"Really, just that. The room was white from top

to bottom, except for two red pillows and a crucifix on the wall. Even the wall art was white. How's the lamb?"

"Oh, it's good—cooked to perfection. So what do you make of all of that?" Slade put a forkful into his mouth.

"Don't know just yet. Her home was almost wiped clean of any trace of personality. It's as if she's hiding from herself in there. Or hiding herself from every-body else."

"You said, 'Almost.' "

"You're listening."

"Always listening to you, Wintahs, always."

I smiled at my friend, and our eyes met for a moment. "I say, 'Almost,' because I found an area—a room, rather—in her house dedicated to prayer."

"Oh, yeah? Another white room?"

"Well the walls were white, but not the furniture or fixtures in the room."

"What was in the room?" Slade took a sip from his glass of wine.

"A table, a chair, a lamp, a kneeler, a glass of water, a bottle of pills, and a Bible."

"Did you say 'a kneeler'?"

"I did."

"Haven't seen one of those in, well, since high school. What do you make of that? Wait a minute, how'd you find this room, anyway?"

"Oh, a self-guided tour." We both smiled at my reply. "But, to answer your question, Slade, the kneeler, along with everything else, told me she might be a bit anal—controlling."

"Okay, anything else?"

"Well, remember what I told you that she told me in the hospital about her sister, Dane?"

"That she was the spawn of the devil, Beelzebub's twin sister, Lucifer's wife? Yeah, I remember that."

I couldn't help but let out a deep chortle at Slade's detailed description. "Something like that. Anyway, according to her, today there were no problems. They just weren't close—one big happy extended family."

"Which story do you believe?"

"It's been my experience that the sedated mind doesn't really know how to lie too well. But you wake that very same person up, and he or she could be the biggest liar this side of the Mason-Dixon. She lied to me today. Still doesn't mean that she had anything to do with what went on at that house, but she lied."

"Might just be a liar."

"Maybe. But one thing's for sure. I'm certain she's hiding something. I also know, though, that most of us have secrets we'd protect with a lie that don't involve murder."

"Got that right. Maybe it's something she just doesn't want folks to know about. Or maybe she's just a big fat liar."

I shook my head and smirked at his blunt characterization. "What?"

He feigned innocence.

"Plus de vin?" François picked up the chilled bottle and offered more wine.

*   *   *   *

My mouth was hurting with laughter at Slade's take on life as I sipped the last bit of wine from my glass.

"That's right, Wintahs, most of the good stuff is either bad for ya, not legal, or jus' downright too wrong to be right. You know what I mean?"

"I know what you mean, Slade. I know what you mean."

"I got a million of 'em, Wintahs."

"You have to stop. I can't take it anymore." I laughed aloud and wiped away the tears. "Why did we wait so long to do this, Slade?"

"Wintahs, I'm not gonna assign blame or name names, but I'm thinkin' it might be your fault."

I roared with laughter again. "Stop. Oh, my God, I haven't smiled or laughed this much in a long time."

"In all seriousness, Wintahs, gotta tell ya, I haven't had this much fun in, well, I don't know when. This is long overdue, I guess, for both of us."

He gave me a prolonged stare that penetrated my heart. This time, though, I didn't look away. I met his gaze with the same affection. Even though we had both sent our representatives out on the date, the real Slade and Morgan took over. Everything was easy, relaxed. We were comfortable being ourselves.

I looked around to see the wait staff stacking chairs and removing tablecloths. Slade looked at his watch. "Hate to say it, Wintahs, but it's gettin' kind a' late."

"Yeah, I guess so. We're the last ones here."

"You ready?"

"I guess," I reluctantly replied, not wanting the evening to end.

*   *   *   *

Earth, Wind and Fire's "Love's Holiday" was in the mix as I leaned back, closed my eyes, and enjoyed the music and the ride home.

"I don't know what the word is out on the street, Wintahs, but I need to let you know something," Slade told me as I felt the car stop. I opened my eyes to see him looking at me. Then he leaned in closer. "This is a date, and it's not over until Morgan and Slade *say* it's over."

He had pulled up to a local live music-and-dance hub, Club Maison. "I love this place, Slade!"

He beamed with pride at his plan as we walked into the eclectic mixture of old and new establishment. The hostess held up two fingers over the loud music. Slade gave her back the universal sign for peace as she escorted us to a table near the dance floor.

"You like?" my date asked.

"I like. I like a lot," I told him as his infectious grin penetrated my core.

"What can I get'cha?" a scantily clad, pretty young waitress stopped by our table to ask. Slade looked at me for my answer to the server's question.

"You know what?" I resolved. "I'm going to have a Kahlua and coffee, extra whipped cream. What the heck, I'm on a date."

"That's what I'm talkin' 'bout, Wintahs. O'Doul's for me."

"Comin' up," the waitress told us.

"You hear that, Wintahs?" Slade asked me as the pulsating, rhythmic chords of Stevie Wonder's "Don't You Worry 'bout a Thing" banged through the room from the live band.

"Oh, yeah," I responded, swaying to the tune.

"That's my song, Wintahs." Slade began to bob to the music. I raised an eyebrow. "What, Wintahs? Don't look at me like that. I might surprise ya." He shot back his crooked smile.

"One Kahlua and coffee for you, and an O'Doul's for you!" the waitress yelled over the music as she served us our libations.

"Keep the change," Slade told her as he dropped some cash on her tray. My taste buds sang as I took a sip of the hot coffee liquor drink. Slade took a swallow from his beer, and then gave me a rascally grin.

"What?" I asked him.

"Told ya, Wintahs. I might surprise ya." He held his hand out to me.

"Oh, this is going to be good." I put my hand in his as he led me onto the floor. He reached for the small of my back and gently pulled my body close to his. *Oh*, I moaned internally. I had never been close to Slade in that way. His rock-hard body was full, comforting, and warm. *This is good*, I thought as we moved in sync to the soul of Stevie Wonder.

*   *   *   *

"Well, I guess it really is that time now," I told Slade as we pulled up to my home and the exhaustion from the long day began to set in. "I had a great time, Slade, and this was a great date."

There it was again—that compelling crocked smile of his. "It was, wasn't it?" he told me as he turned the engine off and looked my way. "You're the real deal, Wintahs."

Our eyes met with eager warmth. He leaned in. But a light from a passing car flashed between us, halting the inevitable moment.

"Boy, those are some bright lights," I chimed in through the moment.

"Yeah, they are, Wintahs, but not as bright as the smile on your face when you laugh."

"You make me laugh, Slade," I told him, as he seemed to covet my being. He leaned in again, this time lightly pressing his soft, full lips against mine. I inhaled at the touch, and exhaled once apart.

"Let me walk you to your door?" he whispered. The rugged gentleman was out from his side and onto mine before I could fully open the door. "I got you, Wintahs." He extended his hand as I stepped out of his black F-150. We walked hand and hand to my front door.

"This is nice, Slade." I turned to face him as we

stopped under my porch light. The moon's reflection on his brown eyes was hypnotic. My stomach tingled with nervous excitement. I was a breathless school-girl again.

"We've waited a long time for this, Wintahs." He held my chin in one of his massive hands and gave me a kiss that sent a stream of desire through my veins. He raised his mouth from mine to look in my eyes. I wanted more—and so did he. I dropped my bag, and we fully embraced. He probed the inside of my mouth with passionate mastery. "I want you," he whispered as his lips grazed my earlobe. "I want you *now*."

๛ CHAPTER 13 ๛

I opened the door to a warm New Orleans breeze. Dawn had just broken, but a thick fog hung around, blocking the sun. This was the first day since the accident that I felt good enough to go for a run. The black leggings and white tank I was wearing seemed like almost too much. I was hot. *It'll be good for the workout,* I told myself as I bent my leg back and stretched to the smooth baseline of Mary J. Blige's "Just Fine" in my headphones. I was headed for one of the many New Orleans levees. This one sat on top of the Mississippi River, a mile or so from my home.

Thirty minutes into my run, and there it was. I had hit my stride—that euphoric, pain-free, feel-good rush kicked in, the runner's high. Just then, though, the music in my ears was silenced by the sound of my phone ringing. I debated on whether or not to pick it up. But it was so early—who would be calling me at this time of the morning?

I scoped the caller ID from my wrist. 'Ivy Carlisle,' I read as my jog slowed down to a walk.

"Ivy."

"Yes, Doctor, I just received a call from the airport. My husband's back in town."

"Got it. Are you okay?"

"I'm perfectly fine."

"Good. I'll see you in the office in a few days for your appointment."

I disconnected the call. *Excellent!* I thought as the funky guitar of Bruno Mar's "Runaway Baby" was next up on my playlist, and began to blast in my ear. But just as I got my feet moving again, the music and my run were interrupted once more. Again I glanced at the caller ID, but this time my lips broke into a smile.

"Slade," I panted his name as I answered the phone.

"Where ya at, Wintahs? Would that be me takin' your breath away?"

"Don't start, Slade."

"What?"

"You know 'what.' Don't make me laugh."

"But that's what I do, Wintahs."

"Speaking of what you do, you can give Redmann Steele a call. I just got word that he's back in town."

"Done. Gonna try to make it happen as soon as possible, then. Tomorrow at six good for you, if it's good for him?"

"Absolutely. Wait a minute. You called *me,* Slade. I know you didn't call about Redmann at this time of the morning. How may I help you?"

"Oh, yeah—well, I figured you were up, and I just called, to say I had a good time with you. I just called to say it was a blast." (He was singing, very badly, to the tune of Stevie Wonder's "I Just Called to Say I Love You.") "Really, Wintahs, just wanted to give you a holla'. Make sure you're following doctors' orders over there."

"Doctors' orders?"

"Yeah, Dr. Slade's orders."

"Well, Dr. Slade, if your orders were to take a morning run on the levee, I'm your best patient, 'cause that's what I'm doin', and I'm lovin' it."

"Good to hear, especially being that you're my only patient." I couldn't help but laugh out loud.

"What am I going to do with you, Slade?"

"Whatever you want," his raspy voice whispered.

"See you tomorrow at six?"

"Tomorrow at six."

"Runaway Baby" was back at it again in my ears. *Doggone it! There he is again,* I said to myself as I suddenly noticed the same blur of a man attempt to quickly scurry off down the levee. *Not this time!* Resolved to confront the man, I picked up my pace to a full-on sprint.

"Hey!" I yelled. The clouds had moved on, and the sun was in its glory, adding to the heat and the number of people on the levee. More than a few runners were between the mysterious stalker and myself, but I was determined not to let him slip away this time. "Hey!" I yelled even louder, as the oddly conspicuous trench-coated man could run only so fast.

I finally reached the would-be lurker. I stood in front of him, bent over, gasping for breath, halting his progress with my hand. "Why are you following me?" I demanded. "I know who you are, and I know you've been following me. What do you want?" His familiar face made itself known as the winded old man looked up at me. "Why are you following me?" I asked him again.

"I don't mean you any harm."

"That's what you said when you came to my house. You stalking me *is* harming me, whether you mean to or not. What do you want? I'm going to ask you again. Why are you following me?"

The old man's frailty was evident, not much to his thin frame. "I just needed to know that you were okay, Morgan."

"What?"

"I needed to know that you were all right."

"What are you talking about?"

"You know me as Calvin Jones, but my real name is Clevis Pitre."

"Clevis Pitre, Clevis Pitre." I couldn't place the name, but the feelings associated with his name were strong, familiar, and disconcerting. "Clevis Pitre!" I exclaimed in resounding revelation. Suddenly the old man's bloodshot, weary eyes fired through his long unruly red eyebrows in piercing recollection. I took a step back, remembering him and those eyes as if it were yesterday. "You! What the hell do you want from me? Haven't you done enough?"

"All these years, Morgan, I've felt so bad for what you saw. I been through a lot. Every time I saw you, all I wanted to do was tell you how sorry I was. But I kept losing my courage. That's all I wanted to do. I just wanted to tell you that I was sorry. That's all. I just want to tell you that I was sorry for making you a part of what I did all those years ago. You don't have to worry about me bothering you again."

I stared him down in silence. His eyes futilely begged for forgiveness. I wasn't ready, though. I was clearly angered by his presence and the memory it brought back. A bevy of emotions welled up inside of me, all vying for space, but anger reigned supreme. This was a part of myself I had walled off from almost everyone, including myself.

I glared at the apologetic, frail old man with hostile contempt. I took a step closer to him, tightened my lips, and, in the chilliest of tones, made my point. "You know what, Mr. Pitre? I'm not the one you need to be apologizing to. But since you're here, I'll take that apology and give it right back to you. 'Cause I don't want it. Now, hear me loud and clear. Leave me alone. I don't want to see you again. If I do, I'm calling the police, and I will press charges this time. That's a promise, and I keep my promises."

"I won't bother you again. I'm leaving town." With that the feeble-looking old man walked away.

*   *   *   *

"This is so good. Your best batch yet." I was sitting at my kitchen table, having just scoffed down the last few morsels of my mother's gumbo. The spoon clanked against the porcelain bowl like a cowbell as I attempted to avail myself of every drop.

"You say that about every batch, dear, but I'm glad you like it," the elder Winters responded on the other end of the phone.

"Boy, I tell you, Mother—shame and secrets."

"What's this about shame and secrets, dear? And am I on that, Alexa? You're talking awfully loud."

I wiped the linen napkin across my mouth, and proceeded to the kitchen sink with my dishes. "I'll call you right back, Mother. Alexa end call." I grabbed my cell and manually dialed. "Better?" Mother hated talking on speaker-phones about what she perceived to be important conversations.

"Much. Now, you were getting ready to tell me something about shame and secrets?"

"Yes, I was. They're such the driving forces of so much pain."

"Yes, they are, but what are you talking about specifically, Morgan?" Mother asked as I sat back at my kitchen table.

"I'm pretty certain that the deaths of Dane Quinn and those two kids were about secrets—people hiding from painful truths. Aaron Quinn pulling a gun on his father, at the core, was about secrets, and stuff folks would rather tuck away for good than talk about, or deal with. We're all as sick as our deepest, darkest secrets, Mother."

"I'm sensing that there's something else going on, Morgan. What is it?"

I pensively sat for a moment, debating with myself whether or not to reveal what happened. I lost the mental coin toss, or won, depending on how you look at it. I decided to set myself free with this one. "You're right, Mother. There is something else."

"What is it, sweetheart?"

"I ran into Clevis Pitre this morning."

"Clevis Pitre! Where?" Mother uncharacteristically shot back in surprise.

"On the levee while I was jogging. But actually, Mother, I'd been seeing him for quite some time. I just didn't know it was him." I heard crickets chirping on the other end of the phone as the senior Winters sat in quite disbelief. "Hello?"

"I'm here. Just taking in what I just heard."

"I understand. All of this kind of put me in a different place, too."

"What happened when you saw him, Morgan?"

"Well, I found out that he'd been watching me for a while. Not too long ago I had an unwelcomed visitor at my home. That unwelcomed visitor was also an over-attentive security guard at one of the office buildings I frequented downtown. Anyway, I called the police on him for trespassing, and that was the last I heard of him—so I thought."

"Go on."

"Well, recently I'd been seeing a man hanging

around my office. He was at my last lecture, too. So when I saw him this morning on the levee, I confronted him. That's when I found out who he was—that it was Clevis Pitre, not Calvin Jones. A lot of years have gone by, and he looked very different from what I remembered. I guess prison will do that to you. But his eyes were the same, Mother." My stomach churned a little with the recollection. "Said that he just wanted to apologize to me."

"Apologize? Humph."

"My sentiments exactly. I had a few choice words for him: at the top of the list, 'Leave me alone'; second, 'If I see you again, I'm calling the police.' Eventually he walked away."

Mother and I sat for a moment as she once again took in what I had just told her.

"Two things," she finally said. "First, have you talked to Commander Slade about this?"

"Yes—well not about this morning, but he knows what's going on. What's the second thing?"

"How did it feel after all those years to see him again, Morgan, the man that you saw molest your childhood friend?"

Dr. Vivian Winters knew how to sit in the uncomfortable quiet and wait for the truth, so we sat for more than a moment.

"I was angry. I was pissed. I was mad at him for

invading my life all those years ago with that vile act. I'm angry at him right now for forcing me to relive the shame and guilt I felt from what I saw him do. I feel it, Mother, just like it was yesterday. And, no, I didn't forgive him."

"Morgan Jane, do you think that it might be time for you to deal with that?" She threw that out there as only my mother could.

I wanted to say no, but I couldn't, for the obvious reason. I agreed with her. *I don't believe in coincidences,* I thought. *So it's not happenstance that Clevis Pitre reappeared in my life at this time. It's time for me to deal with this.*

* * * *

The white woven French linen sheets on my king-sized bed were covered with ballistic, police, autopsy, fire reports, and my dog Maslow in his corner. The TV was running QVC. I had just emerged from the shower and donned my most comfortable white tank and baby-blue satin boxers. My dark brown hair swirled down my back into a working ponytail. I was set. The events of the day had me in full emotional deflective mode. I wanted to forget that I had seen Clevis Pitre. So what's the best way for me not to deal with something? Deal with something else. Fill up every inch of my brain with that something else. And this was a good something else—an important something else. I had a murder to solve.

"Let's start at the beginning," I said out loud, within earshot of Maslow. "The fire incident report." I opened the thick manila folder to paragraph after paragraph of neatly organized information:

> Initial scene survey observed extremely hot and fast moving fire traveling towards the rear of the home, sleeping quarters. Severe fire and smoke damage to Bravo/left side of the home. Hallway, first point of clearing. First body found off hallway, in master bedroom, in bed, on her back. Second and third bodies found in next bedroom, in bed, face down. Clearing began in the hallway, where first body was found. Charring in the roof structure, unusually extreme and deep, is inconsistent with typical fires. Near the rear door of this hallway, a spill or flow pattern was observed. The fuel filter of the furnace was loosened, leaking fuel. Spill pattern was noticed from this area. Possible cause of fire. K-9 did follow a scent.

"Okay, that's the proof that the fire was started on purpose, hence, murders were committed," I pondered aloud. "Now, who did what? Who shot Dane, and who set the fire? Are they the same person? Did the same person that set the fire put that bullet in Dane's head? What about the kids? Who would want to do that? So, what do we have here? Well, we have a fire, or rather, an explosion, and at least three people, that I know of with a motive and/or opportunity."

I placed three index cards on my king-size pillow,

side by side: one for Aaron Quinn, one for Donovan Quinn, one for Redmann Steele. "Let's see," I continued. "Aaron hated his mother. Seemed like she wasn't too fond of him, either. He'd just found out that Donovan was not his father. And, he was there the night of the party." I wrote the four events on four index cards and placed them under Aaron's name. Moving on: "Donovan Quinn, I don't have a motive for you, but I do place you at the scene that night, depending on when Dane was actually shot. And you did have access to your son's gun. You get two cards. And we have my former publisher, Mr. Redmann Steele. You make the list because of your bad dreams, and the fact that you were there. But I'm only going to give you two cards. I'm going to add one more, though: Ms. Kassidy Kane. Why? Because she was there."

One of my Jack Russell terrier's ears perked up. "What's that you say, Maslow? So were a hundred other people. But she's got a secret she's not telling. And for that, she gets a card. I don't see her killing her niece and nephew, though."

I yawned and looked at the clock. It was two a.m. "Maslow, the lack of a witness here is nothing less than problematic for any prosecutor. And where's the gun used to kill Dane? Wait a minute." I grabbed the police report from the Quinn home:

One nine millimeter shell casing found in master bedroom.

I rummaged through some papers to find Dane's autopsy report:

Gunshot wound of close range of fire; projec-
tile – a copper jacketed bullet is recovered and
sent to ballistics; caliber, to be determined; fa-
tal and only wound found.

I tossed around a few more pages on my bed. Ballistics test report:

Weapon type: 9 mm handgun; Cartridge/projectile type: 9 mm
Parabellum.

Once again I went through the mound of papers and
folders on my bed. "Ahh, there it is." It was the police
report from the night Aaron Quinn had terrorized his
father at UNO:

A nine millimeter weapon was retrieved from suspect.

"What a coincidence. Wait a minute. I don't believe in
coincidences. That's the same gun, Maslow."

I looked at the corner of my bed. My dog was fast
asleep. I yawned again. This time, though, I shoved
the papers and folders to one side of my bed and laid
down. The rush of satisfaction I felt from putting the
pieces together was what I imagined a drug fix felt
like. I stared at the pretty lady selling a Dooney and
Bourke Pebble, Leather Brenna Satchel on QVC.

"Call now," was the last thing I heard as I peaceful-
ly drifted off to sleep.

CHAPTER 14

"Is that you, Doc?"

"It's me, Kendall. Good morning," I sang to my secretary as I took in a whiff of the freshly brewed coffee. "Oh, that smells good."

"Well, good morning to you, too, Doc. Here ya go."

I reached for the cup and assumed my position in one of the waiting-room chairs. "Who do we have up first?"

"Well, your nine o'clock is Mr. Duplantis, but he called and said he was going to be late."

"Oh, okay."

"It's a good thing, Doc. 'Cuz a Miss Kassidy Kane left a message saying she wanted to see you this mornin'."

"When?" I stood up immediately and walked over to Kendall's desk.

"She called and left a message yesterday evenin'. Said she wanted to see you today, this mornin', if she could."

"Call her, Kendall. Get her in here ASAP."

"On it, Doc." Kendall scanned the information on the pad next to the phone and started dialing. "Hello, may I speak to Miss Kassidy Kane? Ms. Kane, Dr. Winters has an availability this mornin'. How soon can you come in?" I took a sip and listened. "Very well, Ms. Kane. We'll see you within the next half-hour."

"Yes!" I cheered.

"Kassidy Kane. Now why does that name sound so familiar, Doc?"

"That's the lady that totaled my car on the CCC."

"Oh, yeah. She's gonna be seeing you now, Doc?"

"Well, I'm not certain about that. You know, I'm working on the Quinn fire-slash-murder with Slade now, and Ms. Kassidy Kane is Dane Quinn's sister."

"What'chu say? Mrs. Quinn and the lady that ran into you are *sisters?*"

"Yes, they are. I stopped by her home over the weekend to talk about the case, or whatever she felt she wanted to share. But she wasn't forthcoming about anything. In fact, Kendall, I would say that she lied to me."

"Really? What was it, Doc? Her body language? Was she sniffin' and scratchin' her nose? How'd you know? And what'd she lie about?"

"Actually, she didn't do any of those things. She was very controlled—too controlled."

"*Too* controlled?"

"Yeah, too controlled. Her every move was calculated, to the point of disbelief in sincerity. So when she said to me, that she couldn't remember anything from the night of the fire, I just didn't believe her. I still don't believe her. I'm relying on my senses with this one. The more she talked—or, rather, *didn't* talk—the more I came to believe she was hiding something. Who knows what? Could be anything, right? Secrets."

"You got that right, Doc. God rest her soul, but I remember what Mother Franklin used to say about secrets." Kendall paused for a moment and looked toward the sky. "Mother Franklin used to tell me that keepin' secrets is like castin' a fishin' line in the lake for money. Ya gonna get somethin', but you not gonna get what you want." Kendall sat back and basked in the confidence of her Mother Franklin-ism.

"I completely agree, Kendall. In other words, hiding a secret will bring you immediate gratification, and the false sense of security of control, but it won't bring you what you want, which is peace. Ultimately, our secrets keep us. They bind us. They scare us. They shame us." I drifted off for a moment and flashed back to my own painful secret that I had allowed to keep me for so long.

"Hey, where'd you go, Doc?"

"Huh? Oh, I was in the past Kendall, in the past." My secretary twisted her mouth and frowned her brow with curiosity. "Is this Mr. Duplantis' folder?" I asked her as I refocused my mind's eye and reached for the folder on top.

"Sure is, Doc."

"Very well, then, I'm going to go into my office and review his notes."

"Okay, Doc, and I'll let you know when Ms. Kane arrives."

I flopped my Italian Croco leather satchel on the desk, kicked my gray pumps off, sat in my chair, and took a cleansing breath. I relaxed for a moment, closed my eyes, and reflected on the last couple of days. Suddenly, my mind felt Slade's lips against mine, the smell of his cologne, his hands on my back. I let out a reflective moan, but my phone went off, disturbing my caesura.

"Well, good morning," I greeted the welcomed caller.

"It most definitely is, Wintahs. How you doin'?
"He couldn't see my smile, but I know he knew it was
there. "What's going on over there, Wintahs?"

"Can't say the same ol' now, can I, Commander
Jackson Slade?"

"No, you can't. Oh, by the way, I ever tell ya that I
like it when you say my name that way?"

"What way are you talking about, Commander
Jackson Slade?"

"Whoa, *that's* what I'm talkin' 'bout!" my partner
told me in his most excited growl. I couldn't help but
chuckle at his over-the-top response.

"Oh, really?"

"You know it."

"Too much. By the way, I'm glad you called. I got
something for you."

"I'm all ears."

"I figured something out last night."

"Okay, shoot."

"Perhaps the gun Aaron used to spook his father
with was the same gun that was used to kill his mother."

"How ya' figure?"

"They're both nine millimeters, Slade."

"If that's the case, good catch, Wintahs. I'll see if I can't pull some strings to get a ballistics examiner to run a report. If the bullet casing, or the bullet itself, matches Aaron's gun, we're one step closer to the perp. Also, we got Steele comin' in today at six. You got anything else?"

"Well..."

"Still all ears, Wintahs. What'cha got?"

"The other day, when I was out jogging..."

"Yeah?"

"...I ran into Mr. Jones again."

"Mr. Jones?"

"Calvin Jones, the guy I told you I'd seen following me."

"Oh, yeah. You saw him again. What happened?" I could hear the tone in Slade's voice shift to one of concern.

"Nothing, really. Just told him to stop following me and to leave me alone."

"Not buying it, Wintahs. I know you too well. There's more to this story. And I know you well enough to know that you didn't just tell him to stop following you."

I had hoped to get away with telling Slade that the problem was fixed, without telling him any details.

No such luck, though. Of course, he was right. He did know me too well. Just then, though, my intercom light began to flash.

"You're right, Slade. There is more, but Kendall's buzzing me, and my first client's here."

"We're not done here, Wintahs. Gimme a speed-dial on your phone. You see him again, call me!"

"I hear you."

"Got it?" Slade insisted.

"Got it, Commander Jackson Slade."

"Aw, see now, there ya go." We both chuckled.

"We'll talk later, Slade."

"Most definitely."

"Yeah, Kendall." I hit the red button to end the call, and then my intercom.

"Ms. Kane is here, Doc."

"Send her in."

*   *   *   *

Her appearance was different from the last time. She looked more like the well-put-together lady from the party, but there was something different about her. I couldn't figure out what it was. Her cold black hair was pulled into a sleek, tight ponytail. She had no makeup, except for a cherry-red lipstick. She wore a crisp white dress shirt, khakis, and black pumps.

"When my secretary told me you called this morning, I was surprised," I told her. "Tell me, what brings you here this morning?"

The lines of concentration deepened in Ms. Kane's eyebrows as she sat across from me. It was clear she was still trying to figure out whether or not I could be trusted with whatever it was she was holding on to.

"I remember being hurt and angry that night, the night of the party." Ms. Kane paused and took a deep breath as I listened. "I was hurt because Donovan ended our relationship earlier that evening." She told me this with little or no eye contact.

Didn't see that coming, I thought as I maintained my calm and continued to listen.

"We'd been having an affair for the last ten years. For nine of those ten years he'd been promising me that he would leave his wife, my sister. For ten years I listened to his stories about how awful their marriage was, and how much of a shrew she was. I accepted his guilt-ridden gifts, his late-night calls, his leftovers, and what amounted to his lies. The car that I crashed into yours was a gift from him. He paid my salary. He paid the mortgage on my home. For ten years, I admit today, I was a kept woman. But the night of the party, all that came to a crashing halt."

"What happened the night of the party?"

"That night, the night of the party, I confronted him," Ms. Kane continued with very little eye contact.

"Confronted him with what, Kassidy?" I took the liberty of addressing her by her first name.

"I confronted him with the fact that he'd been see-ing someone else." She gave me direct eye contact. "A woman always knows, doesn't she?" She looked away again and began to tell more. "I am aware of the iro-ny of what I just shared with you, Doctor—a mistress confronting her lover for cheating on her. I hear the insanity. But I am the cliché. I loved him."

"How did you find out about the other woman?" I asked Ms. Kane as the clarity about who it was that sat before me became more and more apparent. *She's been hiding herself, and the low sense of self-worth that would allow her to be with him in that way, for a long time. She derived a false sense of worth from the exterior, his gifts, his promises, what other people saw,* I began to deduce.

"His other mistress left a very explicit note in his coat-pocket. It fell out one day when I picked up his jacket. His response was classic. Every word, every sentence pretty much ended up being, 'Are you going to believe your lying eyes, or are you going to believe me?' For once I chose to believe my lying eyes."

"For once?"

"I know how crazy this sounds. That wasn't the first time I caught him cheating."

"How many other times have you caught him?"

"More than I can count. The other times, I'd allowed myself to believe what I wanted. And I wanted him to be mine. But this time, for some reason, I wanted him to admit it, just once. I was fed up. That night, I did something I'd never done before."

"What did you do?"

"I threatened to tell my sister about our relationship. I threatened to tell her everything. But instead of admitting what had been going on, he got furious. He said the most hurtful things to me that night. He finally told me that he was never going to leave his wife for me, and that we were done. Said he stood to lose too much if he left her, and that I wasn't worth it. I couldn't believe what I was hearing. I just remember begging and pleading for him not to end the relationship. Doctor, when I met Donovan, I was Dane's shy, homely, reclusive older sister who never finished her education. He showed me the world—in secrecy, of course. I couldn't imagine my life without him. I'd become so dependent on him for everything. Anyway, I guess none of that mattered to him. He told me I wasn't worth the expense or the headache anymore, then the part that sent me out of my mind."

She quickly wiped a lone tear that fell from her eye. I handed her a box of tissue. "Thank you." She dabbed her eyes. "He told me that he didn't love me.

Said I was a 'good time' but 'the fun was over.' He told me that I needed to move on, that he had. Then he fired me. How pathetic is that?"

Ms. Kane's brow furrowed as her countenance went from hurt to anger and personal disdain. *Boy, he did a number on her,* I thought. *What a piece of work.* "Yep, told me to find another job," she affirmed.

Ms. Kane and I sat quietly for a moment as she huffed a couple of times in hurt and anger, catching her breath. "I struggled with the sin of this for years, Doctor. But I rationalized it away. I knew it was wrong. I told myself that Dane, my sister, was a miserable, selfish, cruel, horrible person that didn't deserve Donovan. I still believe most of that about her, but I'm thinking at this point that they deserved each other." She looked off to the side. "Anyway, the rest of the evening was a blur, Doctor. I'd drunk myself into a stupor before finally leaving. I was supposed to take the kids to a friend's house. I didn't, I couldn't. I was so distraught and ill-equipped to handle anything. My heart was broken. It's still broken. The next thing I knew, I was being pulled out of my car, by you, on the CCC. That night, the night I ran into you, I was blinded by tears and pain. I wanted to end it all." She reached for another tissue and quietly blew her nose.

"Where were you going, Ms. Kane?"

"I don't know. I wanted to drive into the river, but I guess I drove into you instead."

"What about your sister?" I asked with the notion

to bring up patient confidentiality, but I single-mindedly told myself, *We can work all that out after she finishes. Good Lord, Morgan. Do the right thing, and the right thing will happen. Okay?* I rebuked myself. "Listen, Ms. Kane, before you answer that, I need to tell you that there are limits to our confidentiality. What I mean by that is—"

"You don't have to say any of that, Doctor. I understand that. I know you work for or with the New Orleans Police Department and whatever I say may be used against me, or someone else. I'm not seeing you as a patient. I'm the lady from the party that ran into you, and I happen to be telling you all of this in your office. But I'm done with hiding. Now what did you want to know?"

"What about your sister?"

"What about her? We didn't get along, but we were civil. And, no, as far as I know, she had no idea that Donovan and I were seeing each other all those years. But I did just say that a woman always knows, didn't I? I don't know. Maybe she did know. If she did, she never let on. Even though we were very careful, there was a part of me that enjoyed the possibility of hurting her in that way. I was always taught not to speak ill of the dead, so I'm going to try to do my best not to do so, but my sister was a monster. I know, I was the one having the affair, but she truly was a cruel, manipulative, self-serving witch of a person. I didn't need her husband to run her down to me. I grew up with her. And I probably disliked her as much as anybody did that really knew her, but I didn't kill her, or my niece and nephew. With that, I'm giving you permission to use this information however you see fit. It is what it is. I'm done hiding."

Ms. Kane looked straight into my eyes and asked, "Do I need to call a lawyer?"

"I'm not the police, Ms. Kane, and *they* might want to talk to you further. But let me give you a word of encouragement. There was a time, not so long ago, that I found myself in a secret ill-advised relationship. I was riddled with shame for who I thought I'd become, and guilt for the pain I'd caused others—you know, the sin of it all. So I hid it, just like you did. For a while I even managed to convince myself that this was a normal way to be in relationship. It wasn't. It isn't, under any circumstance. Eventually, the walls started closing in on me. I couldn't hide any longer, from myself or anybody else. You know the old saying, 'Wherever you go, there you are'?"

Ms. Kane timidly nodded.

"So I stopped hiding and admitted my ugly truth to God, myself, and then a friend," I continued. "By the way, God knew already. He always knows, and he never stopped loving me. I stopped loving myself. After that, I was on my way to setting myself free from that relationship and the shame of my secret. So it's good that you're done hiding, Kassidy. Hiding the sin, the secret, can be worse than the sin itself—oh, that flashing light is telling me my first client is here. One more thing, though, before we close."

Kassidy began to gather her belongings, then stopped to look up at me.

"What made you call?" I asked her.

"Honestly, Doctor, I was going to take this secret to my grave. I was never going to talk about it with anyone. In fact, I'd planned on seeing my grave sooner than later. But perhaps the deaths of my sister, and my niece and nephew, and your words brought me here today."

"My words?"

"Yes, your words. The last thing you said to me before you left my home that day touched a place in my heart. In that moment, somehow, I didn't feel so alone. Do you remember what you said to me?"

"I do. I commented on the scripture your Bible was open to."

"To be exact, you told me that Romans 6:6-7 could be freeing." Ms. Kane paused for a moment. "Doctor, did you know that there are one thousand one hundred and eighty nine chapters in the Bible?"

"No, I can't say that I knew that," I answered as I weighed her words.

"Well there are. Every morning at 7:05, I read approximately three and three-quarter chapters of the Bible per day. Within a year's time, I will have read it in its entirety. Then I start over again. I know, I've been told that I can be a bit anal at times. I've been doing this for a year and a half now. But after the accident, for the first time I'd gotten behind. I couldn't get past Romans 6:6-7. I just couldn't turn the page. I kept reading it over and over again. Every morning, I'd wake up with the intention of reading and turning that page, but I couldn't. It began to feel like everything else in my life—wrong. Other than taking my own life, the possibility of freedom from the pain seemed futile."

That would explain the Ambien, I thought as I remembered the bottle of sleeping pills on the table beside the Bible.

"But your unsolicited statement about Romans 6:6-7 was blunt and divinely inspired," Kassidy continued. "It tapped into what little motivation I had left to do anything other than, quite frankly, die. So when you left that afternoon, Dr. Winters, instead of swallowing a handful of pills, I picked up my Bible and read that scripture one more time: *"We know that our old self was crucified with Him in order that the body of sin might be brought to nothing, so that we would no longer be enslaved to sin. For one who has died has been set free from sin."* Soon after I read those words, the feelings of worthlessness began to lift. I was able to turn page after page, gaining some sense of personal value and, yes, freedom. But more importantly, that night I realized I wasn't *living* at all in the sin or sins I was committing. I was dying a long, slow death."

Ms. Kane dabbed what appeared to be a tear from the corner of her eye.

"There is nothing for me to add to that, Ms. Kane," I finally said. "If you want to see me again, you have my number."

CHAPTER 15

"Name?" asked the same blank-faced, unaffected woman behind the Plexiglas window at St. Paul's Mental Facility.

"Dr. Winters."

"Who are you here to see?"

"Aaron Quinn."

"Ma'am, I don't see your name on the list." *Here we go again,* I thought as I plotted what I would say. I thought again and decided to just keep it real.

"I'm with the New Orleans Police Department, investigating a crime." I showed her my badge.

"Through the double doors and to your right. Take the elevator to the third floor. Punch in this code." She handed me a small piece of paper with four numbers on it. "He's in Room 307." Without hesitation this time the gatekeeper gave her spiel and buzzed me through.

With ease this time I made my way to Aaron Quinn's room, and there he was. Except for the scraggly beard, he looked the same. His pale complexion matched the cold, sterile room as he once again lay handcuffed to the metal railing of the bed.

"Aaron?" I quietly called his name.

His dark eyes opened wide and alert immediately. "Oh, it's you." He closed his eyes again. "What do you want?"

"I want the truth, Aaron." I thought I might be able to softly strong-arm him into the truth.

"What are you talking about? I haven't lied to you."

"Oh, but I think you *did*, Aaron. You're either lying by omission, or you're just lying. Which one is it? You said the gun you had at UNO the other night had never been used. That wasn't true. Was it?"

"What are you talking about? I never used the damn gun. Hell, I was afraid of the thing. The only time I *thought* about using it was to take my so-called father out. I never used that gun."

"How did you get the gun?"

"Why? What do you want from me, Doctor? I'm already locked up."

"I want the truth." I looked straight into his round, dark eyes. "I'm pretty certain that it's the same gun that was used to kill your mother."

The young Quinn rolled his eyes in complete irritation. In that moment, I realized he wasn't lying. "I have nothing to lose or gain from lying to you," he said. "I snuck back into the house the morning after the fire and took my gun, along with a few other things. It was exactly where I always left it. If it's the same gun, somebody else used it. I didn't."

At this point the irritation in Aaron's eyes went artless and remote. He really didn't have anything to lose. I believed him.

*   *   *   *

I walked through the front doors of the precinct, and there he was, standing at the water cooler, just inside the door. As far as I knew, Redmann had no idea I was going to be at the police station. He didn't see me, though. I usually liked to be just a little late for these interviews. The surprise factor was a good tool. So I closed the door and loitered outside for a few minutes.

"Hey there, Doc," said Officer Leblanc. "How's it goin'? I hear you and the boss got an interview today."

"Yeah, we do. How's the wife and kids, Leblanc?"

"Oh, you know, Doc, same ol'-same ol'. You comin' in?"

I peeked through the open door. Steele was gone. "Yes, I sure am. Thank you." I allowed Slade's team member to hold the door open as I walked through.

"Good seein' ya, Doc."

"Good seeing you, too. Tell your lovely wife I said hello."

"Will do."

As Leblanc left my side, I stopped by the water cooler and tarried to give Slade and Redmann extra time with each other. Oddly enough, and as many times as I had questioned people for the NOPD, my stomach churned just a tad at the thought of interviewing Redmann. I chalked it up to the fear of the unknown. I knew his personality type could be very unpredictable—volatile, even. *It's time, Morgan,* I told myself.

Ringing phones and loud conversations filled the air as I walked down the corridor of the busy precinct. I could hear Redmann's big laugh through the walls as I stood outside Slade's office. *He's laughing. Good.* I knocked on the door.

"It's open." The two men were sitting next to each other in front of Slade's desk. Good-cop, bad-cop had already been established, so the cheerful conversation he and Slade were having before I came in was good to see.

"Wintahs, we were just sittin' and talkin' about the last time either of us saw a possum around here. Mr. Steele here says he saw one the other day at the airport. You believe that?" The two men chuckled at their semi-private joke.

Slade already seems to have his trust, I thought as Slade stood and began to walk toward his desk.

"Mr. Steele?" Slade began.

"Please, Commander, call me Redmann."

"I can do that, Redmann, and you call me Jackson."

"Very well. I know I don't have to introduce the two of you. But I was just gettin' ready to tell ya that Dr. Wintahs here was gonna be sittin' in today. No big deal, though. Y'all know each other already, right?

"Hi, Redmann, I'm just going to take this seat," I said.

Steele's smile diminished as I sat next to him. In fact, his demeanor completely changed from open and pleasant to closed and protective. He folded his arms and almost puffed himself into a bigger, wider person. His brows furrowed just enough to secure his personal border. He was on the defense. "So, what can I do for the two of you?"

"Well, Redmann, we're pretty much interviewing everybody that stayed late after the party," I began. "So tell us everything you remember from that night."

Steele frowned and tightened his lips as he seemed to ponder the question. "So tragic, what happened and all. To tell you the truth…"

Uh-oh, I thought upon hearing those words and noticing Steele's eyes veer up and off to the right—an indication that he was about to use his imagination in whatever he was about to say.

"…the evening was such a complete joy of an experience, it's so hard to fathom what all took place later that night for my good friend Donovan."

Maybe I got that one wrong. Doesn't sound like creativity there.

"Same here, Redmann," I said. "I could say the exact same thing. But is there anything about that night other than how much everybody seemed to enjoy themselves, and what unfortunately happened later, that you remember?"

Steele turned away from me to face my partner. "I can definitely tell you this, Commander. I didn't hear a gunshot. I don't remember seeing anyone or anybody suspicious. Everybody and everything seemed to be good." My former publisher wanted to let me know he did not appreciate my presence. And he was not going to give me the respect of addressing me directly.

This is such child's play, I thought. He seemed to further barricade himself, only granting me a cold smile from time to time. His tactics were old and classic: divide and conquer. To what end, though? Was this his attempt to change the dynamic in the room, pitting Slade against me? Or were these simply more antics, derived from his passive-aggressive tendencies? Either way, I knew not to take any of it personally. I briefly made contact with Slade, subtly nodded my head and raised my eyebrows, signaling him to take over. *Patience is the key.*

"So, ahh, Redmann, how long you been knowin' the Quinns?" Slade began.

"It's been about five years now. We signed our first contract with Donovan in 2012."

"Is that right? What about the rest of the family? What about Dane? Did you get to know her at all?"

"Can't say that I got to know her that well, Jackson." For the first time, he made little or no eye contact with Slade.

"But you'd met her before, right?"

"Oh, yes, certainly. She seemed to be a lovely person. But I spent far more time with Donovan. We had a great working relationship. I've found his professionalism and sense of work ethic to be second to none. I remember countless times that I wondered how he was able to put in so much time?"

Oh, no. He's trying to change the conversation. "Can I circle back to Dane for a minute, Redmann?" I inquired. Steele rolled his eyes like a child as he turned back my way. "Tell me about the last time you remember talking to her."

He took a deep, annoyed breath. "Not much to tell, Morgan. It was a conversation full of cordial niceties. The kind you give acquaintances."

He's really not going to like this question. "Redmann, did you talk to Dane the night of the party?"

"What do you want from me? Yes, I talked to her the night of the party. She was one of the hosts."

"What was that conversation like?"

"Look, I've answered your question, Morgan. I told you I didn't really know her that well. Now, what's your next question? I have things to do." His attempt to contain his anger was betrayed by his flared nostrils, shallow breathing, and tightened lips. His reaction to the questions about Dane were obviously out of whack.

Slade sat quietly behind his desk. Suddenly, though, the shrill of a loud siren went off. Officer Leblanc burst into the office. "Boss, sorry to interrupt, but we're on lockdown again. You know the drill. Shelter in place."

Redmann's face twisted with fear.

"It's probably nothing," Slade told us as he proceeded to lock the door. Then he peered through the blinds, with his hand hovering over his firearm.

"What's going on, Slade?" I asked as my heart began to thump just a little faster through the continued piercing blare of the siren.

"A perps is on the loose, or lost," he said mat-ter-of-factly. "This is protocol until he's officially se-cured, found, or accounted for. It's probably nothing, but we can't take any chances."

I saw Redmann's blue eyes grow large and strained. "Redmann, are you okay?" I asked him as he seem to continue to unravel. His face and lips, now panic-stricken, were almost completely void of blood, white with distress. He didn't answer. He couldn't. His breathing was suddenly shallow and intense. "Red-mann, talk to me! Are you okay?" I asked again, over the blaring siren.

"I'm fine, I'm fine," he muddled through his own panic while clutching the arms of his chair.

"You don't look fine! Are you in pain?"

"No! I don't know," he breathlessly told me as beads of sweat poured from his forehead.

"What's going on here, Wintahs?" Slade interject-ed. "Is he all right?"

"No, he's not! This looks like a panic attack!" I con-tinued to yell over the siren. "Redmann, take a deep breath!"

"Oh, my God! Oh, my God!" He released one of the arms of his chair, and grabbed his chest.

"You're okay, Redmann!" I insisted as the siren continued to sound. "You're having a panic attack! Give me your hand!" His eyes shifted back and forth in petrification. "Give me your hand, Redmann!" He did. His paw was cold and clammy as he squeezed my hand. "Now look at me! Look at me, Redmann!" He managed to focus his gaze on my eyes. *If I could get him to pay attention to me, it'll distract him from the mania in his head.* "Now breathe. Listen to the sound of my voice, and just breathe. You are okay. You're going to be fine. Just breathe. That's right, breathe in, and out." I inhaled and exhaled with him.

"I'm going to die!" he shouted. "I have to get out of here! I have to get out of here!" His eyes darted about again in frantic alarm.

"Redmann, breathe. You're *not* going to die. You're going to be okay. Breathe. Look at me. Look at me."

The siren finally stopped. Steele began to look around the room for the noise that was no longer there. His breathing slowly stabilized. He jumped in fright as two raps on the door broke the sudden quiet. "All clear, boss," said a voice on the other side of the door.

"Keep breathing, Redmann. Keep breathing."

I noticed Slade's hand still hovering over his gun. Eventually, though, he shook his head at the event and finally relaxed his posture. "How 'bout some water?" he proposed.

"That would be good, Slade. Bring two, please."

"I don't know what happened," Steele said anxiously. "That's never happened to me before."

Slade poured a couple of glasses of water from the black-and-gold pitcher sitting on his desk. Steele now seemed to be flushed with embarrassment as he let go of my hand, and the color began to return to his face.

"From the looks of things, it seems as though you had a panic attack, Redmann," I told him. "Lots of people have them."

"I thought I was going to die."

"That's kind of what a panic attack will do to you."

Slade handed us the glasses of water. I made eye contact with him, signaling a changeup. Without a word he slowly disappeared into the corner of his office.

"And that's never happened to you before?" I asked Steele, who looked away, this time with a shame-filled expression. "A lot of people suffer from panic attacks, Redmann. They're nothing to be embarrassed about. That wasn't the first time, was it?"

"No. They started after the fire. Been hiding them pretty good until today." He looked away, and then back again at me, waiting for judgment. "I'm not like a lot of people, Morgan. I run a multi-million-dollar business. If people outside of that door—my competitors, my enemies—knew about this, I would be considered weak. This *is* weak."

"I hear you. But let me say this to you. We don't really know what the folks on the other side of that door are thinking, or might be thinking, or would think. But we know what you're thinking about yourself. Don't we?"

My former publisher nodded in slight agreement.

"One more thing," I continued. "I know for sure that the people who suffer the most, from anything—panic attacks, addiction, cancer, overeating, depression, you name it—are the ones that suffer in secrecy. So I want to congratulate you."

He curiously looked at me.

"You set yourself free today," I assured him. "You are no longer suffering alone. You're not hiding anymore. I know that wasn't your intention, but you've been given a gift. You didn't tell the world, but you told somebody. Your secret is no longer a secret."

This was the first time in the history of my relationship with Steele that I saw him vulnerable and open. His brutish ways were quieted.

"I don't believe in coincidences, Redmann, I told him, maintaining my calm, soft-spoken voice. "You were *supposed* to be here today, when the station went on lockdown. You were *supposed* to have a panic attack, in front of me. And you were *meant* to come clean about it today. But that's not the only secret you have, is it?"

"What are you talking about?"

"I'm talking about Dane. Tell me about your relationship with Dane. Now's the time, Redmann."

He looked at me and then took a sip of water, as if he wanted to say something. He stared me down, attempting to pull some decision-making help from my eyes. I sat and waited as he hemmed and hawed, struggling to come clean with whatever he was hiding.

"Who was Dane to you, Redmann?"

"She was my..." he mumbled.

"She was your what?"

"She was my lover, dammit! She was my lover. I didn't kill her, though. I didn't want her dead. I loved her."

And there it is. I thought as I listened to him reveal the illicit affair with his so called friend's wife. I was trying my best not to judge, but he had been such a brute, that it was a challenge.

"How long had you been seeing her?"

"About a year." He hung his head, refusing to grant me eye contact—this time, though, for a different reason. He was no longer hiding anything. He seemed to be grappling with either guilt or grief. I couldn't tell. Either way, sadness had taken over his presence. His shoulders were slumped, and what I could see of his face was long and drawn.

"Were you with her the night of the party, Redmann?"

"Yeah, I was with her."

"When?"

"Early on, at the beginning of the party."

"How were things?"

"We had an argument."

"What did you argue about?"

"She threatened to tell her husband about us."

"What made her do that?"

"She did that to get under my skin because I couldn't give her the time she wanted from me. She was like that. When things didn't go her way, she'd threaten to blow up everything."

"What'd you tell her?"

"I told her I'd kill her if she told her husband, or tried to leave me. Even though I hated how he grinned and shinned like he did for everybody, he made us money—lots of it. Told her I'd really blow everything up. I even held a gun to her head."

"What gun, Redmann?"

"The gun in the other room. Is that why I'm here? You found my prints on the stupid gun. I didn't kill her. That's just how we were with each other. She knew better than to mess with me. I didn't hold back, and neither did she."

"How did the argument end, Redmann?"

"How did it end? Like all our arguments ended. We made love. When I left her, she was more than alive. She was satisfied."

I felt a chill as he boldly met my eyes and defiantly smiled at his description of their last encounter. By now, though, he had left his trancelike, vulnerable state. The shield was back up, and the Redmann Steele I knew was back.

"How much longer do I have to be here?" he continued. "Look, if I'm not under arrest—and I'm pretty certain I'm not—I'm leaving. I don't have to talk to you! I don't know what the hell I'm doing here in the first place! I'm getting out of here!"

Steele positioned himself to leave at the door. I looked back at Slade. "Hold on there Redmann," he told him, as he planted himself before the enraged mogul.

" 'Hold on,' nothing!" Steele snapped. "This is bull! You don't have anything on me! This is a sideshow of a police station! I'm not doing this anymore!" He shoved Slade.

"Think again, buddy," Slade retorted. "You just assaulted an officer of the law, and thanks to you, we have more than enough to hold you on probable cause." He quickly manhandled Steele, placing his hands behind his back and handcuffing him over his desk. "You have the right to remain silent. You have the right to an attorney. If you can't afford an attorney, one will be provided for you. Do you understand the rights I have just read to you?"

"I want my lawyer! You can't arrest me!" Redmann's face was twisted with anger. His eyes were blazing with belligerent disdain for anyone in eyeshot. *This is the uncontrollable rage Ivy talked about,* I thought. *Perhaps this is what Dane saw the night she was murdered.*

"Pipe down!" Slade yelled back.

"Everything okay in here, boss?" Officer Leblanc stepped back into the office.

"No, process this clown and charge him with assaulting an officer, for starters."

"Got it, boss." Leblanc grabbed ahold of Steele. "All right, we can do this the easy way or the other way. Your choice, buddy."

"Do you know who I am?" Steele shouted. "Get these handcuffs off of me!"

"Guess we're doin' things the other way. Anders, Glapion, I need a little help here." Leblanc tightened his grip on Steele as the rest of Slade's team rushed in and dragged the unhinged suspect out, kicking and screaming. Slade then closed his office door. We both took a seat and exhaled.

"Boy, that went south in a hurry," he said.

"Yeah, it seemed as though his memory of the night's events triggered a lot of emotion. Guys like that have a hard time dealing with uncomfortable feelings. Problem is, most of their real feelings are uncomfortable to them. They spend a good portion of their adult lives running away from them. They recoil at any type of true emotional connection. So they rarely let folks in. But, every now and then, they let their guards down, like today. But when they let someone in..."

"Like Dane Quinn."

"Like Dane Quinn, that vulnerability leaves them deathly afraid you'll leave them, and they'll do anything to avoid it."

"Anything, Wintahs?"

"Anything. You saw him. He went from zero to a hundred in seconds. That kind of temper, along with everything else, can kill. I tell you, Slade, my intuition is subject to prejudice right now with Steele, but we definitely have ourselves a *bona fide* suspect."

"Yeah, but how would he have done it, if he did it? Everything we have is circumstantial, not a lick of hard evidence, Wintahs."

"My theory: whoever did it, took or used Aaron Quinn's gun to shoot Dane. Then he or she put the gun back into its case in Aaron's bedroom. Then, hours later, maybe as an afterthought—or a forethought, who knows?—he or she set a fire or explosion in hopes of covering up the murder."

"Well, he does have a lot of rotten passion and other stuff goin' on in that hot head of his. Maybe he left a little somethin' out of what he told us today. Like, 'Oh, yeah, and then I shot her in the head.' Whatever the case is, he's lawyered up now, so we've gotten out of him everything he's gonna freely give at this point. Oh, by the way, one day I'm gonna stop wondering how you do it. But did you know about his affair with Dane, before today?"

"No, I didn't know about his affair with Dane, but I knew he knew more than he was telling us. And thank God for precinct lockdowns. That's what brought him to his humanity for a minute. Without the lockdown, which caused his panic attack, I don't know if he would have ever let his guard down long enough to be honest in any way about that night."

"Yeah, I'm pretty certain you had something to do with him letting his guard down. I tell ya, Wintahs, watchin' you dissect that joker, after he did all he could to get under your skin, was something else."

"Yeah, I had to remind myself not to take any of his gruff personally. Then I was able to remember that patience usually avails itself to all sorts of fruit. It was good to see him vulnerable for a moment. But here's my real beef. Slade. He's got enough money to get good help." I sat up and squared my shoulders.

"The best," Slade chimed in.

"The best! There's help out there. No one has to suffer from emotional or mental conditions like that, whatever it is. I see it so often. People stand behind their pride, their fears, and more often than anything else"—Slade leaned just a little closer to hear my last thought—"their guilt and shame."

"Guilt and shame, huh?"

"Yeah, guilt about the ways they've acted out—the things they've done to people, including themselves. And shame about who they believe they are, for having an illness or a personality disorder. But, Slade, if we could just make mental healthcare as common as dental care, the world would be such a better place. You know, good help is right there, especially for someone with his means. It's there if you don't have the means—not the way it used to be, but it's there."

I fell back into my chair and exhaled. "All right, I'm off my soapbox. I'm done. I just had to say that."

"That's deep, Wintahs. But you know what?"

"What, Commander Slade?"

"I agree."

I smiled. "Oh, got something else for you, speaking of rotten passion."

"Out with it."

"Ms. Kassidy Kane stopped by my office yesterday."

"Speed Racer?"

"Yep. She dropped a bombshell, Slade."

"I'm listenin'."

"She told me that she and her brother-in-law have been having an affair."

"Her brother-in-law?" Slade was baffled.

"Donovan Quinn, her brother-in-law," I bluntly stated.

"What?"

"Yeah. Said it'd been going on for years. Ten, to be exact."

"Ten years?" Slade shot back.

"Ten years. Said she busted him cheating on her, and the night of the party she confronted him."

"Oh, boy, that never goes well."

"And it didn't. She said that after he was done denying it, he told her it was over."

"Really?"

"Told her he was never going to leave his wife, and then he fired her. "

"Ouch! What about the other woman?"

"What other woman, as far as he was concerned? Ms. Kane told me he stuck to his story."

"Those lying eyes again, huh?"

"Right. He called her a liar and told her that her services were no longer needed in any way."

"All this the night of the party?"

"Yep. She said that's why she was a drunken mess when she ran into me that night."

"Well, I'll be. Sounds like somebody else with a motive, and access. Wait a minute. How are you able to tell me this? You saw her at your office, right?"

"Yeah, but she made a point of telling me she wasn't my patient, and that she was done with hiding."

"Done with hidin', huh?"

"Yeah, hiding their relationship, hiding her feelings, hiding what happened that night."

"You believe her?"

"I do, Slade. I do."

"You know what, though, Wintahs?"

"What?"

"She just got listed as a suspect in my brain. Got a real pretty motive here."

"Yes, we do, but I don't think she did it, Slade. I saw no signs of deceit from her, like I did the first time we talked at her home. In fact, her steady eye contact reeked of honesty. But I don't know, Slade. She had nothing to gain by coming to me like that, other than a lifted burden. Oftentimes, when a person is truly done hiding and lying, they seek the truth, and the consequences become irrelevant. They just want out of the mental prison."

Slade pensively stared at me. It got quiet for a moment. He went to the white board in his office and uncapped the black marker. "Okay, we have Miss Kane, that hothead Steele that we just locked up, young Aaron Quinn, who's also locked up, and now Don Juan Quinn." He began to write all of those names on the board. "They all seem to have some type of motive, and they were all there."

"Correct."

"We know young Quinn hated his mother and his father. He'd just found out, from his mother, that Donovan wasn't his father. Again, motive, and perhaps opportunity." He continued to write.

"And now the latest twist. Donovan Quinn—"

"Yeah, Don Juan over there has been cheating on his wife for at least ten years, with his wife's sister. And had at least one other woman on the side. Only thing, Wintahs—why would he kill Dane? He put that fire out. He told the troublemaker to hit the road."

"Right. If he was going to kill somebody, you would think it would have been one of his mistresses."

"Yeah, Speed Racer is the one that threatened to out him."

"She did, but you have to account for the unknown factors of the type of person that compartmentalizes like that. We have no idea what else was going on with him and his wife. And what about the insurance policy?"

"Okay, so we know he had opportunity, but no concrete motive."

"And then we have Steele."

Slade wrote 'STEELE' in big all-caps on the board. "Right, we know he was in a passionate love-hate relationship with his so-called friend's wife, the deceased, and he admitted to arguing with her shortly before her death. He had an argument with the deceased, who also happens to be the woman he was having an affair with, the night she was killed. He threatened to *kill* her the night she was murdered, with the murder weapon. And, coincidently, she threatened to out their relationship to her husband that night, too. Lot of threatenin' going on in there. Got a lot of motives. Got just as many opportunities, but very little evidence."

"How long can we hold him for this, Slade?"

"As long as we can. Remember, he did just assault an officer."

"That he did."

Slade capped the black marker.

❦ CHAPTER 16 ❧

"How was your day, dear?"

"Oh, Mother, it was quite the day. Can't say that it was bad. Can't quite say that it was good, either." Phone in hand, I slid into the comfort of my bed and summoned Maslow over. "Come on, boy."

"Well, then, what can you say about it?" Mother continued from the other end.

"I can say that we arrested somebody for assaulting an officer of the law—Slade—and for suspicion of committing the murder of Dane Quinn."

"Oh, my. Is Commander Slade okay? And who was arrested?"

"Slade's fine, and you'll never guess who was arrested."

"Tell me."

"Redmann Steele."

"Your publisher?"

"Former publisher. I'll tell you about that later. But, yes, Redmann Steele, publisher and CEO of Simon & Steele Publishing, admitted to having an affair with Donovan Quinn's wife, Dane Quinn."

"Morgan! No!"

"Yes. Slade and I interviewed him down at the precinct earlier today. He told us that, the night of the party, he and Mrs. Quinn got into a big fight—a lovers' quarrel, if you will. He also admitted to threatening to take her life. And he also admitted to holding the murder weapon to her head. But he did not admit to killing her. He said he didn't do it."

"Don't they all, dear?" I chuckled at my mother's cynical conclusion. "All in all, sounds like a very productive day, Morgan. "You have a would-be killer behind bars, all be it pending further fact-gathering, mystery solved, right?" Her words were meant to be taken as subtle encouragement to dig deeper. We both knew that very few things were that easy.

"I hear you, Mother. We don't have any real evidence that he actually did it, other than his admitted circumstantial words. But..."

"But what, dear?"

"Here's what I think: being removed from that *event*, we might have the wrong man behind bars for murder, but, a little sit-down time for Redmann Steele in the poky was definitely in order. Can't say that I hated seeing him get hauled off."

Mother chuckled at my response. "So what's next?"

"We're going to continue to see where the facts and all these family secrets take us. Tomorrow I have a Donovan Quinn lecture to go to."

"Is that so?"

"Yeah, Slade and I interviewed him a day or so ago. He asked me if I wanted to go. I jumped on it. I'm looking forward to it. Should help the fact-finding go a little smoother. Also, speaking of lectures, the following week I'm the featured speaker at a symposium on shame and guilt."

"That should be good."

"I'm going to talk about what I saw all those years ago."

"Very good Morgan. It takes a lot of courage to come out from hiding and deal with one's own self-doubts and fears, publically. But on the other side of that moment in time, is the reward of full acceptance of yourself. It's not easy, but most things worth having come from a lot of effort. Morgan Jane Winters, I can't tell you how proud I am of you for having the courage to set yourself free. Bravo, dear, bravo."

"Thank you, Mother." I smiled from ear to ear, like that little eight-year-old girl at my mother's encouragement.

"For what, dear?"

"For being Victoria Winters, and my mother."

"It's my pleasure, sweetheart. Now you get some rest, and have a goodnight."

"Good night, Mother."

I put the phone on my night table and lay awake, thinking about what my mother had suggested. "Very few things are that easy, Morgan, and you know it. It's not Steele," I mumbled myself to sleep. "Who else had a motive? Who else? Well, everybody else—Aaron, Kassidy, Steele, all seemed to have a motive. Wait a minute. It's staring me right in the face. I can't believe it. I can't believe it…"

✧ CHAPTER 17 ✧

"Mornin', Doc."

"Good morning to you, Kendall."

"Coffee?"

"Don't mind if I do. Stay seated. I'll get it."

"How'd it go yesterday, Doc? Oh, before you tell me that, Miss Ivy left this message on the machine. I think you might wanna hear it."

"Okay." Kendall put the message on speaker-phone as I poured myself a cup of coffee.

"Doctor, this is Ivy Steele," went the voice. "Although I do believe that I have benefited greatly from our counseling sessions, as of today I am canceling the rest of our sessions until further notice. Take care, and once again, thank you."

"Humph. I'm sorry to hear that." I was concerned about my patient, but I can't say that I was surprised. After all, her husband had just been locked up, and I did have something to do with that. *I'll just have to rely on what she said to me the last time I saw her. She said that she was a survivor.*

"Does this have anything to do with you talkin' to Mr. Steele yesterday?" Kendall asked.

"I can't help but think it does. He's in jail."

"What? What the heck happened, Doc?" She sat up straight and put her coffee down.

"Well, let's start with the fact that the precinct went on lockdown as soon as we started talking."

"Lockdown?"

"Yeah, lockdown. Somebody in custody escaped, broke free, while we were there, and we had to subsequently shelter in place. Then, while the three of us—Slade, myself, and Redmann—were sheltering in place, Redmann goes into a panic attack." I took a sip and shook my head at the recollection.

"Oh, Lawd!"

" 'Oh, Lawd' is right, Kendall. Then one thing led to another. He shoved Slade, and that's when the cuffs went on."

"Go 'way from here! Right there in the Comman-da's office?"

"Yes, he did, right there. But before all that, he had a panic attack, that seemed to bring him to his knees. As he put it, he thought he was going to die. But had it not been for the lockdown and subsequent panic at-tack, I don't believe my former publisher would have revealed that he had been sleeping with his so-called friend's wife, Dane, for the last year or so."

"Oh, no, Doc! Get out! So he did it! He killed her! *Did* he do it?"

"It's possible, Kendall, but at this point I don't real-ly know. He gave us a very small window of vulnerable insight. In the middle of all that, he suddenly realized he was exposed—naked, if you will. And, unfortu-nately, people who experience life in that way live in constant internal petrification and turmoil. They're always hiding, seeking comfort in the fact that they haven't let you in. Ultimately, it's a fear of feeling their feelings, and the natural intimacy that occurs when a person opens up, that drives their actions."

"Sounds like one of them cycles, Doc?"

"Yes, it's a vicious cycle, Kendall. It's his own shame about what he's feeling, is the only way I can explain it. When he hit his limit, he went on emotion-al lockdown and unleashed his inner childhood bul-ly to protect himself. But people with those types of challenges can and do shut down at the drop of a hat. One of the many things they've neglected to deal with on the inside, gets triggered, and bam, gates closed. You know, Kendall, as cruel as Redmann could be, he's no different than so many of us."

"How so, Doc? He sounds kinda crazy, ya know what I mean?"

"I do, and, yes, he is working with the instability that comes from emotional—or rather, mental—illness. I would say Mr. Steele, like so many of us, is trying to wrestle with his imperfections alone. We all have things we need to work out, but not alone."

"You got that right, Doc."

"But I'm going to assume that, because some of us have been so emotionally handicapped or stunted through early life or childhood experiences, we have trouble relating: in Redmann's case, deathly afraid of intimacy, relationships and feelings. For a brief moment during that interview with him I had his trust that I cared about him and what he had to say, which I did. But the minute he began to *feel* a little too long, if you know what I mean, there went the moment of intimacy, the moment of sharing—the moment of truth-telling, the trust. There went the interview."

"They kind of lie about everything, huh, Doc? Pants just on fire all the time. Am I wrong?"

It felt good to chuckle at Kendall's words. "No, you're not. They hide through deflection, projection, denial, by any means necessary. 'It's you, not me,' whatever it is. If done enough, he or she will start to believe his or her own distortions. Boy, I tell you Ken-dall—power, wealth, and insecurity are an ugly mix."

"Goodness, Doc! That must feel terrible on the in-side, huh?"

"I can only imagine, Kendall. When I think about it, it's almost as if they live a life of internal terror, afraid of being found out, constantly testing the waters, and when the slightest pain, discomfort or true intimacy are felt, they either run or attack. The question here is, which one did Redmann do the night of the party? "

"Yes, indeed." We both sipped our coffee. "But how would he have done it, Doc?"

"That's the sixty-four-thousand-dollar question, Kendall. From what he told us, there was no motive, but we don't know that. He was there. He saw her be-fore, or possibly around the time she was killed. He had the time, and the opportunity to get the gun."

"But what about the fire, Doc?"

"What about the fire? That's the question. How could he have set the fire and been outside at the same time? Don't have the answer to that one. Unless..."

"Unless what, Doc?"

"Unless someone else set the fire."

"Who?"

"Working on it, Kendall. I'm working on it."

"Well, Mother Franklin used to say that what you're hidin' from in the dark's gonna be sought after by the light of the truth, like a game of hide-and-seek. Because truth says you'll only find it when you come lookin', but I was right there all the time. 'Cause hidin' your truth is livin' like you're dead, and that ain't no way to live. Just let *that* one sink in, Doc."

"Mother Franklin was right. In the end, Kendall, what he revealed might have circumstantially incriminated him. But I'm a firm believer, as you know, in the truth setting you free. There will be consequences, but it—the truth—will always set you free."

"Amen to that, Doc."

*   *   *   *

"So you're off to your boy's lecture, huh?"

"Yeah, I tell you, Slade, this lecture has taken on a completely different meaning, now that I know about his relationship with Kassidy Kane. I confess, at this point, I don't know him at all. His decade-long affair with his sister-in-law totally caught me off guard. As far as I'm concerned, I don't know him at all. The more I think about it, and the more removed I am from seeing Steele hauled off, the more uncertain I am that he's our man."

"What'cha thinkin'?"

"My gut tells me that my former publisher didn't kill anybody."

"Your gut's been pretty accurate. I'm listenin'."

"Okay, so he goes on angry tirades against anybody that even *suggests* a criticism. He defends himself by putting you down. And, yes, he does create his own reality—lies when he feels threatened. He can be deceptively charming one minute and then out to verbally and spiritually kill with words and putdowns the next."

"Saw both of those guys in my office—the hot one and the cold one."

"Right. They both answer to Redmann Steele."

"Wintahs, ya makin' a good case for the prosecution here."

"Stay with me."

"Not goin' anywhere."

"With all that, Slade, I can't say that he fits the description of this killer. I do think he's hard-wired for narcissism, though, and perhaps traits of borderline personality disorder, too. Many people in power have some degree of narcissism, and some have it as a personality disorder. I think that might be the case with Steele—his grandiose sense of importance, that sense of entitlement and arrogance, to name a few traits. The borderline part speaks to his hair-trigger temper, his hypersensitivity, his unstable relationships."

"The prosecution's lovin' this, Wintahs."

"I know, but in order for me to see him as this kill-er, I would have to see something else that I don't see."

"Maybe the sociopath that couldn't give a flying duck about how me or you might be feeling about what he just said or did?"

"Exactly—and that's certainly not Steele."

"I've been circling Don Juan Quinn in my brain."

"Now *that* one might better fit the title 'socio-path.' He's appeared before thousands, maybe even millions, of people all over the globe as the quintes-sential family man. His mild-mannered, even-keeled demeanor and persona would suggest that he is just that. But, given what we now know, he more fits the description of a non-caring person with a lack of con-science."

"A sociopath."

"Perhaps Slade. He's obviously not the hardened sociopathic criminal we're used to seeing in jail or on the streets. He's refined, good looking, charming, smart. But now we know, that's his representative. God only knows who the real Donovan Quinn is. But if I were to believe what Kassidy Kane told me—and I do—what's on the inside is a manipulative, pas-sive-aggressive, mean, egocentric person. You get the picture. But is he a murderer? Could he have, *did he* kill his two kids and his wife? I don't know. He was there from beginning to end. He had access to the gun."

"But what's the motive?"

"Get this, Slade. Donovan's had all these women for all these years, but pretty much had his steady two, until this mystery woman comes along. Somehow, suddenly, Quinn dumps the one mistress we know about, and then his wife turns up dead. And then, what about the insurance policy? Motive?"

"Motive. But what about the fire? There's no way he could have set that explosion off, though. He was standing outside when it happened."

"True, haven't figured that one out yet. Nor do I see him killing his own children. Unless..."

"Unless?"

"A contractor and collateral damage," we said together.

"After all," I said, "remember, the kids weren't supposed to be home."

"Right. So, who knew that Wintahs? Who knew that the kids weren't supposed to be home? Kassidy, Donovan, possibly Redmann, and maybe Aaron."

"Yep, all the would-be suspects. So where does that leave us? *I'll* tell you where that leaves us. Right back where we started, but with a better profile of who that person might be."

"I know that voice, Wintahs. What'cha got cookin'?"

"Is there any way you could run a check on Donovan, just to see what comes up? We know the renowned author and lecturer. Who else is he?"

"I can do that. In fact, good idea."

"Great! He's hiding more than an affair. I'm sure of it."

"Let me ask you somethin'. Kinda off the topic."

"Shoot."

"What's the deal with this Calvin Jones guy?"

Slade's question was met with silence.

"You still there, Wintahs?"

"I'm here."

"Good. So what's the deal?"

I sat at a red light on Elysian Fields, trying to will the light to change, as if that was going to make Slade's question go away. "Awww, come on, a turn-signal would help! Sorry about that, Slade, but I really don't like it when they don't use their turn-signals." I griped, then took a deep breath and decided to talk to my friend. "Okay, Slade, I'm going to pull over."

"You got time to do that, Wintahs?"

"Yeah, I'm early, and I'm not far from the lake. So I'm just going to turn right here onto Lakeshore Drive. Give me a minute." The clacking turn-signal on my car was suddenly loud and intrusive. I wasn't looking forward to the conversation I was about to have. "What a beautiful day."

"That it is, Wintahs."

I parked my car, rolled my windows down, and watched the small waves wash up alongside the embankment of Lake Pontchartrain. Thanks to my friend's gentle persistence, I decided to have a conversation I had avoided most of my life.

"I was about eight years old, Slade. I'd gotten a bike. I thought that bike was the best thing I'd ever seen in my life—pink tassels hanging from the handlebars, a pink banana seat. I tell you, it didn't get much better at eight. Needless to say, I loved riding that bike. I rode it as far as Mother and Daddy would let me, which was up and down the block we lived on. But eventually I got tired of riding down that one block. You know, it wasn't about the bike anymore. It was now about where I could go, what I could see, and who could see me on my bike. So, being the good little girl that I was, I asked my mother if I could take it little further—you know, go around the block."

I could hear the quiet of my friend's listening ear.

"You've met my mother. What do you think her answer was?"

"Oh, absolutely not."

"Correct—and I was devastated. So I asked again, and again, and yet again, until Mother made it clear that she would let me know when, and not a minute sooner."

I'm was in a good place talking to Slade, I thought, as I took my emotional temperature. I felt no judgement from him. I felt safe, as I always did with him.

"Told me that when I was older, I could ride further," I continued. " 'But for now, you stay on this block,' were her last words. Slade, I pouted like there was no tomorrow. I thought that was the biggest injustice that could ever be perpetrated on *anybody*. You know what I eventually did?"

"I do."

"One day, I just took off. Slade, I remember thinking, 'How old do I have to be? After all, I'm

eight.' "

I could hear my friend lightly snickering on the other end of the phone.

"I thought that bike was the best, but, boy, riding outside of Mother's designated perimeter, you couldn't beat that with a stick. Even the sun seemed brighter off of my block. Slade, I didn't think I could have more fun in life. I rode everywhere I could think to ride, in my new-found freedom."

I paused for a moment to gather my thoughts.

"You still there?" Slade quickly chimed in.

"I'm here."

"Okay, okay, just makin' sure. I was ridin' with ya, Wintahs." His words brought a comforting smile. I truly wish he could have been with me all those years ago.

"Well, it started getting late," I said, "and I knew I'd been gone for a while, so I decided to take a short cut.

"Uh-huh."

"There was a very pretty shaded alley that ran alongside a few houses. Figured I could cut my drive-time a little if I took it, so I did. I turned off the street and into the alley. At the end of the alley, almost sitting by itself, was the Pitre home. I was still in the ally, but because the Pitres' blinds and curtains were open, I could see everything. I remember seeing the biggest oil painting I'd ever seen of the Last Supper in one of the rooms. I can still see it. It practically covered the entire wall. The Pitres had lots of plastic-covered furniture too. I also remember seeing Mr. Pitre molesting his granddaughter, Lacy Pitre, my friend, in the very last room of the house."

"Awww, jeez, Wintahs! I'm sorry." Slade respired as we sat for a moment.

"Yep, unfortunately, I remember it like it was yesterday."

"Kind of hard to let go of a memory like that. Did he see you?"

"Yes, he did. We actually locked eyes for one awful second."

"What happened when he saw you?"

"Slade, I rode home so fast. I rode like hurricane winds. I remember hardly being able to catch my breath."

"Did he ever try to contact you?"

"Yes and no. As luck would have it, that night he was picked up by the police for embezzlement. It was all over the news. Shortly thereafter, the family packed up and moved away. He served a lot of time in the Federal penitentiary. It was my prayer that I would never see him again."

"This might sound like a stupid question, Win-tahs—"

"The only stupid question is the one that doesn't get asked. What's your question, Slade?" I trusted his questions, anyway.

"Why was this your secret? You didn't do anything wrong."

What a thoughtful, kind thing to ask. I reflected on Slade's question. I almost felt like that eight-year-old little girl again.

"Try telling an eight-year-old little girl that she didn't do anything wrong, when she saw her friend being molested, and didn't tell anybody until months later. Yeah, even though he went to jail for a long time, that eight-year-old little girl—me—held onto that sin, almost as if *she* were the molester. What's that saying? 'You're as sick as your deepest darkest secret'—well, *I* was. All my young mind knew was, if I told my mother and father what happened, I was going to be in trouble. After all, I'd disobeyed her, and look what happened. I'd concluded that this is what happens to disobedient little girls. So I said nothing. I hid it from everyone. I hid what I did. I hid what I saw. I hid how I felt. I hid everything, Slade. I put myself in that shame-filled isolation. For years I racked my brain trying to figure out how I could have helped my friend."

"You were a child, Wintahs. You were victimized, too." Slade's caring words were so soothing and reassuring. Tears began to well up in my eyes and choke my voice.

"Yeah, I know, Slade, but try telling that to an eight-year-old little girl. And here, we have the beginnings of a young child's unholy foundation of shame." I stopped for another minute and looked out at the choppy yet calming lake water. "Eventually I came out from hiding. One day, the ultimate God-given truth-seeker in my life, mother, sat me down and assured me that, no matter what was going on, she wouldn't leave me, she would always love me. That day I revealed my secret and set myself free. Much like I'm doing right now."

"Humph."

"Oh, I almost forgot. Clevis Pitre is also Calvin Jones."

"Kind of figured that. That's some story, Wintahs. If you don't mind, though, I'd like to reinforce your verbal restraining order, and make sure he's gone."

"Don't mind at all. I didn't feel threatened, nor do I now, but no harm in putting an exclamation on that point for him to stay away. Anyway, Slade, it's about that time. I need to get to the lecture. I can't thank you enough for your compassionate ear."

"Anything for you, Wintahs." His husky whisper sent a stream of warmth through my veins.

"Any chance of you stopping by the lecture this evening?"

"I don't know. Depends on how fast I can get rid of this stack on my desk. But I'll push your request for info on Quinn to the top of the heap. I'll text ya if I find anything on him."

"Call me later?"

"Try to stop me."

↞ CHAPTER 18 ↠

"He's one of the most dynamic speakers of our time. We're honored to have him here…"

I walked in to hear Donovan being introduced, quickly making my way backstage. He was off to the side of the stage, behind the curtains, waiting to go on. His assistant, Lola Mendez, was standing in front of him, picking lint off his jacket.

"Donovan, hey." I gave a loud whisper as he turned my way.

"Morgan! Good to see you. So glad you were able to make it." We cordially embraced. "You remember my assistant, Lola Mendez?"

"Of course. How are you, Ms. Mendez?" This time there was no sting. It was nice to see her. She was wearing the same beautiful pashmina I had seen her in the night of the party.

"I'm well, Dr. Winters. Thank you for asking." The dark beauty's eyes quickly traveled the length of my body, with an assessment. "He's almost done, Dr. Quinn. Here's your water." She handed him a bottle of water and brushed his shoulders.

The room was packed. I wondered how many people were there for the actual lecture, versus the number of people that were there to see the man behind all the terrible drama. Either way, Donovan usually packed them in.

"Folks, let me present to you Dr. Donovan Quinn." The facilitator lauded as the auditorium filled with applause, and Quinn began to make his way to the podium.

"Good evening, everybody..." the lecturer began to the full house.

"Looks like he's doing well, considering all that's he's been through," I told Ms. Mendez. "Wouldn't you say?"

"I would, Doctor. Yes, I would say that." She and I stood side-by-side backstage, watching Quinn greet the crowd.

"How long have you been working with Donovan, Ms. Mendez?"

"I haven't been with him that long—a couple of semesters. I'm so sorry, Doctor, but I'm going to have to dart off. I see Professor Comeaux over there. I've been trying to track him down to get the summer seminar schedule for Dr. Quinn. I have to catch him."

"Please, no worries, Ms. Mendez," I told the eager assistant as she quickly left my side to tend to business.

"Make sure you catch the end, Dr. Winters. That's my favorite part."

"Absolutely."

Some fifty-five minutes or so later, my phone went off. I scurried away from the stage. "Dang it! I'm going to miss the end!" I whispered out loud as I rummaged through my bag for the phone. *Dropped call. Doggone it.* It was Slade. The building we were in was notorious for having poor reception. He said he would text if he found anything. *Call him later, Morgan. I want to hear the end.* I went back to the curtain to hear what was left of the lecture.

"...How can you fix someone else's life if you haven't fixed your own? It's just that simple, folks. I tell people all the time that the way to bliss, the way to happiness, the way to a fixed life is through the fire. You can't bump into it—you have to break into it. You have to go through it. You gotta dip into it. You have to look into it. Folks, you have to undo, review, and renew. There's only one way to *what?*" Quinn cupped his ear with his hand for the audience to shout back the phrase.

"Fix your life!" the crowd shouted back as Dono-van took a sip of water, stood back from the dais, and flashed that undeniable grin. Applause, as well as a standing ovation, swept through the room. He took a bow and began to walk off the stage, then paused as he noticed me.

"Yeah?" he trumpeted to the crowd. Being in eye-shot of me, he gave me the thumbs-up.

"Yes!" the crowd shouted as I reciprocated his af-firmative hand-gesture with a thumbs-up. He went back out to take an encore bow. He knew how to work a crowd. No denying it—he was good, and his mag-netic charm was on full public display.

"Thank you! Thank you!" he told the plaudits as he walked the length of the stage, waving to the guests. My phone buzzed again, this time with text messages, startling me away from my scrutiny of Quinn.

This better be good, Slade, I told myself as I began to read his messages:

> Quinn not on record at Boston State U.

> Quinn has aliases; Donovan Fontenot; Donovan Smith; and Don Jenkins.

> He's a gambler; In debt; He's...

The applause finally seemed to die down. I looked up in unprepared surprise to see that Donovan had left the stage and was making his way toward me. My phone was still buzzing with more text messages from Slade. I wanted to read them, but I didn't dare risk it—not in front of Quinn.

"How was it?" he asked me as he got closer. I quickly stuffed the phone into my bag, trying to play it off. *This has got to be the loudest silent-mode cellphone ever,* I thought. I could still hear it vibing deep down in my bag.

"You got the hot line there, huh, Morgan? Something important?"

"Oh, no, that's just my secretary sending me some info on an upcoming trip. But first things first, Donovan. That was great! I loved it, especially the end." I was doing my best to divert him away from my attention-seeking phone.

"You know, that's what everybody says. They tell me they love the end. Like I told you, though, Morgan, it's not easy doing this, but it keeps my mind occupied."

"How do you do it, Donovan? I know how much energy this takes. How do you do it?" I continued to stall, trying to compose my mind, though I knew Quinn wasn't on the up-and-up about everything. I didn't expect what I had just seen on my phone.

"Dr. Quinn, we have some folks here that would like to have a word with you, and have you sign their book." Event attendees had gathered at the end of the stairs leading up to the stage, waiting on a chance to speak with the famous author.

"Oh, go ahead, Donovan, I can wait," I told him with insistent relief.

"You sure?"

"Absolutely. I'll be here."

"Who do we have here?" he said to the first person in the receiving line as he turned on the charm. He was good. I watched him effortlessly glide in and out of conversation with his admirers. Quinn and everything I thought I knew about him had taken on a different meaning, though.

Who was he? I thought as my phone continued to buzz with messages. I stepped off to the side. Seven messages! *Goodness!* I thought as I read:

> Call me. Be careful. Don't confront him until I get there. We don't really know who he is.

Slade, you know me better than that, I told myself as I walked just a little closer and turned up my bionic ear to hear Quinn's conversations.

Some fifteen minutes later, a pretty young brunette with big brown eyes stood talking to him as the last one in line.

"And, I'm sorry, what was your name again, dawlin'?" Quinn asked her with his usual allure.

"Sherry Ledet," the young woman answered, as I continued to watch and listen.

"Sherry Ledet, What a beautiful New Orleans name. Miss, or Mrs.?

"*Miss* Ledet. I'm not married." The young woman giggled.

"A beautiful woman like you? Can't be true."

She gazed at him with the infatuated eyes of an innocent yet welcoming fan. He reciprocated her stare with eager eyes and a toothy grin. He was now two completely different people, his charm in full effect, as opposed to the appropriate, well-behaved gentleman I had just interacted with. The flirtation between the two was palpable. Even though Quinn was always a little overly complementary, he was never inappropriate, or even flirtatious, with me or others in my presence.

Suddenly, though, he looked over his shoulders, as if to see if anyone was watching. I tried to look away as quickly as I could, but his eyes caught mine before I could. He turned back to the young lady, but his demeanor had immediately changed.

"Morgan, if you don't mind, come over here."

"What's that, Donovan?" I feigned.

"Please, come over. I have somebody here that wants to meet you. Miss Sherry Ledet here is too shy to ask herself, but she recognized you when you came in, and wanted to meet you."

I dropped the phone into my bag and made my

way over to Quinn and the young lady. "Miss Ledet, meet Dr. Morgan Winters."

"Nice to meet you, Ms. Ledet."

"Oh, Dr. Winters, it's an honor."

"I told her that you were good people and that she didn't have to be shy," he said, "even though you're one of the greatest psychological minds around."

Oh, he's good, diverting my attention away from his behavior with complementary words while handing Ms. Ledet the token largesse of meeting me. He's good. "Well, Ms. Ledet, it certainly is nice to meet you," I told her cordially as the house lights were being turned off. "Oh, boy, looks like we're the last ones. We're going to have to get out of here before they turn all the lights off." We all looked around at the empty auditorium.

"Miss Ledet," Quinn continued, "if there's anything I can help you with in the future, you know how to find me, right?"

"Yes, I do, Dr. Quinn." The young lady left the stage area and went on her way.

Quinn and I appeared to be alone in the auditorium, but I was almost certain we weren't. Security is always lurking until everyone is gone. "Walk with me backstage, Morgan," he said. "I left some of my notes back here."

"Certainly, Donovan. I'm so glad you asked me to this lecture."

"Me, too."

"It's as if I'm seeing the real Donovan Quinn for the first time. You know what I mean?"

We stopped for a moment as Quinn looked my way and rapidly blinked his eyes with confusion. "Can I ask you something?" We resumed walking behind the barely lit backstage area.

"Yes," He reluctantly agreed.

"How is it that you were able to keep your relationship with Kassidy Kane a secret for so long?" Yeah, I went for it. *This type of personality doesn't react to hand-holding honesty,* I thought. *He reveals when he's forced to, or caught off guard, which is a rarity. He's a con man. He's always plotting his next move, and how he can use someone or some circumstance to his advantage. This man does very little, because his heart told him to, or by accident.*

"What are you talking about?"

"Can we be honest? I know all about it, Donovan. I just want to know how you were able to keep it a secret for so long."

Quinn was at a rare loss for words. We were standing close enough in the dimly lighted area for me to see a streak of panic in his eyes. I caught him off-guard.

"I don't know what you're talking about, Morgan." He began to walk faster. "Where's my folder?" He attempted to digress as I gently tugged at his arm.

"Donovan, wait, talk to me," I lightly insisted. "It's just the two of us in here. How were you able to do that for so long?"

"I'm going to tell you again, Morgan. I don't know what you're talking about." This time he snatched his arm back from me and began to walk away.

"Well, maybe Donovan Fontenot might know the answer?"

Quinn stopped dead in his tracks and slowly turned back toward me. His unspeaking, insolent eyes penetrated through the shadowy room as a quake of panic now swept through *my* body. His angry reaction jarred loose my tunnel-vision of solving this crime. Suddenly, my thought process was taken over by the realization that I might be standing with a cold-blooded killer. My stomach turned as I looked around and took in the reality that we truly seemed to be alone. I didn't see a soul.

What the hell were you thinking Morgan? I chastised myself. *You've just pissed off a man you suspect of being a murderer. Is this what you would tell someone else to do? No! You better get out of here. Run!* I yelled in my head, all in a matter of a Nano-second. *Calm down, calm down. Breathe, Morgan, breathe, God, I'm asking for your wisdom here. Take away this fear, and let your will be done, not mine. Hopefully, your will evolves me getting out of here alive.*

I took a couple of passive deep breaths, and the fear was gone.

"What did you say?" He tightened his lips and crisply annunciated every consonant.

"I said, perhaps you'll answer to Fontenot. What about Smith, or Jenkins?"

Quinn huffed and puffed in red-faced anger. "You're not going to ruin this for me!" he belted. "Why are you doing this, huh? I've worked too hard for things to end like this. What do you want from me to keep quiet, Morgan? I have money. Is it money that you want? I have a big insurance policy getting ready to hit. It's worth millions."

I found it odd that he would offer me money for my silence. Angry as he was, why didn't he threaten my life, if he was the killer?

"What do you want?" he continued. "Why are you doing this? Wait—you think I killed my family, don't you? That's what this is about. You think I shot my wife and suffocated my children. Don't you?"

I looked at him for a break in what I perceived as his act. There was none. "I honestly don't know," I replied. "I do know that nothing's adding up, Donovan. In fact, things are multiplying." I took my phone out and began to read from it: "Don Smith, Donovan Jenkins, and Donovan Fontenot. Boston U never heard of you; your gambling debt; sleeping with your dead wife's sister, and whoever else. Who are you? Did

Dane know who you were? Is that how she ended up with a bullet in her head?"

Quinn paced the floor, holding his head in his hand, realizing that perhaps the jig was up.

"Look, Morgan, I got in some trouble when I was young, so I changed my name a few times. All right, I don't have a Ph.D. from Boston University. I haven't been the greatest of husbands. And I like the ponies. But I didn't kill anybody. Those were my kids that died that night." His shattered voice echoed through the empty offstage area. I noticed he was still telling me as little as possible about that night, but I believed what he was saying.

"Did Dane know about your past?"

"She did."

"When did she find out?"

"Years ago, when we bought our first home. I tried to hide it from her, but eventually she put a private investigator on my tail. He uncovered everything. It's amazing what people find out with a little effort."

"She was okay with that?"

"Hell, no! She threw it in my face every chance she could get. But she insisted we stay together. She blackmailed me. Said that if I ever thought about leaving, she'd make sure that everybody knew about my past. Said that she would ruin me."

"Why would she want to stay?"

"She said that I was a gold mine, and that I was going to make us rich. She was right. She knew I had a gift for making people believe whatever I wanted them to believe. She was a miserable human being, and I hated her. I cheated on her with as many women as I could. And, no, she had no idea how much debt we were in. I hid that from her. Look, I wanted her dead, but I didn't kill her. I'm not a killer."

I believed him. "Well, if you didn't start that fire and kill Dane, Donovan, who did? Who else hade the time, motive and opportunity? Who else had access to your son's gun? Can you think of anybody else that was there that night who might have had the opportunity? Anybody?"

Quinn shook his head and frowned his brow in confusion. "No, I can't."

Gotcha! I said to myself. *He's lying.*

"You're not telling me the truth," I told him. "I believe you when you say you didn't kill your wife and kids. But, I don't believe the words you just said to me. I'm not a lawyer, but we have a lot of circumstantial evidence here, and it doesn't look good for you. Whatever you're hiding can't be any worse than you going to jail for murdering your family, especially if you didn't do it. Now I'm going to ask you again. Are you sure there was nobody else at that house when the explosion went off?"

Quinn rolled his eyes and twisted his mouth in consternation. He appeared to be weighing the question. "My assistant was the last person to leave the house." He paused and eyed me—to judge him, I guess. I had done that already. At this point, all I wanted was the truth.

"And..."

"After everyone left, she met me outside, and we had a meeting in the back seat of Dane's Maybach," Quinn told me with a blank face that quickly turned to one of self-impeachment. His eyes drifted toward the floor. That was the first time I had seen even a semblance of honest remorse from him.

"What happened after your meeting?"

"My house blew up."

"What about your assistant?"

"I told her to leave, and she did."

"Your assistant? Are you talking about Lola Mendez?"

"Yeah."

"I saw her earlier. You have any idea where she is now?"

"Here I am, Dr. Winters," said a voice from the dark.

"Lola?" Quinn yelled, as we both looked around.

We couldn't see anything. The sounds of footsteps from the opposite side of the stage made themselves known as a silhouetted figure slowly came into focus.

"Yes, it's me, Lola." She was holding a shiny silver pistol.

Any time now, Slade, anytime. "Ms. Mendez?"

"Yes, it's Ms. Mendez, and I heard everything."

"Lola, sweetheart, I didn't know you were still here," Quinn nervously chimed in.

"I guess you didn't," she said. "But I am, and I heard everything. So, I'm not the only one." Ms. Mendez said, as she let out an anguish filled laugh. "I don't believe this. How could you do this to me? How could you do this to *us?* I thought you loved me, Donovan. You've been sleeping with Ms. Kane? You told me you loved me. Was it all a lie?" Ms. Mendez longingly looked at Quinn. "Of course it was. I've been such a fool. How could I have thought... You told me we were going to be together forever. You told me that the only thing keeping us apart was your wife. I betrayed everything I knew to be right for you. I would have done *anything* for you. I did the *unthinkable* for you, and *you lied to me!"*

Her eyes were fiery, full of contemptuous hurt. Quinn looked at me in frustrated bewilderment and decided to take a stab at talking her off the ledge. Unfortunately, though, he was who he was, which meant more of the same. "Lo, you know I love you. Those other women didn't mean anything to me. You're the one in my heart. It's just you and me, Lo. I made a mistake."

"Do you hear, that Dr. Winters? He made a mistake, a *mistake*." Ms. Mendez threw her head back in ominous, hurt-filled laughter. "You *accidentally* slept with me, your sister-in-law, and countless other women, by 'mistake.' That is funny."

"Lo."

"*Shut up*! Just stop, Donovan. Just be quiet."

"Lo, baby, sweetheart, listen to me, baby. I love you..."

I don't believe it, I thought as I observed Ms. Mendez's eyes apparently softening while Quinn professed his love.

"How I want to believe those words, Donovan," she told Quinn as tears began to fall from her eyes. "But I know now. You're a liar, and I don't believe a word you say." She suddenly stiffened her upper lip and began to compose herself. "All of this is going to be out in the open. Make sure you tell everyone, Dr. Winters—no more secrets. It's over now. It's all over. The two of us are really going to be together forever, just like you promised. I'm going to keep your word for you."

Quinn's eyes reeked of petrification as he looked toward me for help. Sensing none was forthcoming, he turned back to Ms. Mendez. "Lo, baby, listen to me. I love you." I touched his arm to quiet him, as she seemed to be on the precipice of shattering any shred of control that she had left. Her words were life-ending.

"Goodbye, Donovan. I love you."

BANG! Ms. Mendez shot Quinn squarely in the stomach in a maelstrom of agony, and then held the gun to her own head. His mouth fell open in shock as he placed his hand over the wound. He pulled it away, and looked at the bloody mess, validating his disbelief. "You shot me!" He glared at his mistress, then looked at me, and slowly fell to the hard floor.

"Now it's my turn," she said.

"Lola!" I shouted. "Lola!" I screamed louder, with success this time, as her glassy distant eyes met mine. "Lola, he's not worth this. And you're worth so much more than this. You really are. He did a lot of terrible things to you, but don't let him take everything from you. Put the gun down. Put it down. Don't leave here like this. I know this is not what you want. Look at me, Lola. Look me in my eyes."

She held her gaze with mine.

"You don't have to do this. He's not worth it, but you're worth living for. It's never too late to do better, no matter what you've done last month, last week, yesterday, ten minutes ago. As long as you have breath, you have the grace of being able to make another choice, a better choice. It's never too late, Lola. Look at me, Lola. It's never too late."

I held on-to her eyes with mine as tears began to fall. She slowly began to lower the gun, eventually dropping it to the floor. She then fell to her knees in tears. I rushed over to Quinn, removed the suit jacket I was wearing, and draped it over his shoulders.

"Hold on, Donovan. It's going to be all right." I knelt at his side and used my hands to apply pressure to his wound. "We need to get him to a hospital, Lola. He's losing a lot of blood."

She was unresponsive as she continued to rock back and forth on her knees, crying. I reached my bloody hands into my bag for my phone. "God, let him pick up," I said out loud as I multi-tasked, tending to Donovan's wound, while keeping an eye on Ms. Mendez. She continued to rock on her knees, mumbling to herself.

"Yeah, Winters, I'm on my way."

"While you're at it, get an ambulance here ASAP. Got a man down with a bullet to his abdomen."

"What the...? You okay?"

"I'm fine. I'll explain it to you when you get here." We hung up.

"Lola! Lola!" I yelled. She slowly looked up. "I need your help! He's going to die! I need your help!" She reluctantly tore herself away from her misery, got up, and walked over. "Put your jacket over his legs." The up-close-and-personal shock of what she had just done left her paralyzed as she stood over us. "Lola! Put your jacket over his legs. We need to keep him warm. And give me your scarf." Quinn began to shiver, and Ms. Mendez eventually knelt on the other side, placing her coat over his legs, as she handed me the scarf. I placed it over the wound to help stop the flow of blood. Her face began to soften as she looked at the man she had just shot, the man she had professed to love.

"I only did it because I loved you. I love you so much. I didn't mean for them to die. I did it because I love you. I didn't know they were going to be there." She lightly stroked the side of his face as he gasped for air.

"What did you do, Lola?" I asked her as I continued to apply pressure to Donovan's wound. The blood vessels in her face began to dilate as she blushed with the sadness of shame. "What did you do the night of the party?"

Lola looked up, stared off into the distance, and began to solemnly recall what happened. "I watched Dane go upstairs early in the evening. Then I watched Redmann Steele go up after her. Something told me to follow him, so I did. When I got upstairs, I could hear arguing coming from the master bedroom. It was the two of them. I listened outside the door. They were saying the meanest, most hurtful things. He threatened to kill her. The door started to open, and I hid again. I saw him go into Aaron's room. He came out with a case in his hand and went back into the master bedroom, where Dane was. I went back to listen at the door. They argued again, but the next thing I heard were the sounds of two people making love."

Donovan coughed. Ms. Mendez continued to stroke the side of his face. "When they were done," she continued, "I watched him come out of the bedroom, tucking his shirt in and zipping his pants. I'd had enough. I couldn't stand the way she treated him. I couldn't stand the fact that she was keeping him from me. I went in to confront her. I opened the door, and there she was, the great Dane Quinn, sitting on the side of the bed, putting her shoes on. She just looked at me."

"How did she look at you?" Lola turned away from the space that captured her vision and glared at me dead-straight in the eye.

"She looked at me like I was nothing, like I was a piece of scum on the bottom of her shoe, like I was trash. She *always* looked at me that way. I hated the way she looked at me. I told her what I thought about her behavior and that Donovan deserved better. She laughed at me. She told me that I didn't know what I was talking about. She told me to make myself useful, get out of her bedroom and go fetch something."

Donovan managed to reach out with one of his bloody hands and touch Ms. Mendez's hand. "I'm sorry," he whispered through muffled moans and groans. Lola put her other hand over his, looked at him with sorrow, and continued to speak.

"That's when, all of a sudden, something came over me. I saw the gun lying on the bed. She saw me looking at the revolver. She dared me to use it. She told me that a weak-minded piece of trash like me didn't have the guts to do anything with it. So, I picked the gun up and shot her in the head. She'll never look at me like that again."

A tear trickled down Donovan's cheek as he listened to his mistress describe how she killed his wife.

"Then what did you do, Lola?" I asked her.

"I wiped the gun clean with that." She gestured toward the pashmina I was using on Donovan to help keep him alive. "Then I put it back in its case and brought it back into the other bedroom." She looked down at Quinn. "We were going to be happy, like you said. Just you and me."

"What about the fire?" I gently demanded, wanting all the pieces to the puzzle.

"What about it? My father was an HVAC man. I knew how to start a fire from a furnace. After I'd taken care of Dane, I loosened the fuel filter of the furnace and let it drip through the evening. By the time I went back upstairs after the party, there was oil everywhere. I lit a match from Dane's bedroom. Soon thereafter, an explosion. I didn't know Donnie and Ashley were home. I didn't know." She hung her head in self-recrimination.

Finally, I said to myself. At long last I heard sirens at a distance. Though the fear I had initially felt for my life had long since been over, I was more than relieved to know that the cavalry had finally arrived while Donovan was still breathing.

"Wintahs!" Comfort echoed through the empty auditorium to the tune of Slade's voice. "Wintahs!" he yelled again.

"We're behind the stage, Slade!" *Thank God!* I said to myself as the kata-kata of footsteps made their way closer and closer. Slade and his team—Glapion, Anders, and LeBlanc—trampled in with guns drawn.

"You okay, Wintahs?" He had an unusual look of disbelief on his face.

"I'm good, Slade." I gestured my head toward Donovan. "*He's* not so good, though. Ambulance here?" I was growing weary of the task and blood at hand as I continued to apply pressure to Donovan's bleeding wound.

"Yeah, yeah, they're right behind us. What the hell happened here, Wintahs?" Slade looked at me, Donovan, the gun, and then Ms. Mendez, who sheepishly averted her eyes from him. "Lo?"

"I'm so sorry. I killed them. I killed them. I'm so sorry. I'm so sorry... I didn't know the kids were there. I didn't know they were there. I'm sorry."

"What?" Slade blinked and frowned in bafflement

as the EMTs arrived.

"We got it, Doc," an emergency worker said as he took over for me. Slade helped me up and gave me a handkerchief for my bloody hands. Ms. Mendez continued to apologize almost incoherently.

"She shot him, Slade."

"Huh?" Slade's eyes were still in disbelief.

"She shot him, she killed his wife, she set the house on fire, and she killed his kids. She was Quinn's mistress."

*   *   *   *

I sat off at a distance in one of the auditorium chairs. Donovan was being wheeled out on a gurney. Ms. Mendez was sitting on a chair on the stage, handcuffed. Slade was standing next to her. She didn't look as if she was saying anything, though. Eventually he patted her on her shoulders and signaled for his team to take her away. I walked over, meeting him halfway.

"You okay?" I asked him.

"Yeah, *I* should be asking *you* that."

"No, as you can see. I'm good. How'd that go over there?" I was referring to the conversation Slade appeared to have with Ms. Mendez.

"Oh, that. Couldn't really ask her anything or talk to her. You know, she was read her rights. Besides, she was kind of talkin' out of her head. Just sad, Wintahs, anyway you look at it."

"Agreed."

"Just…"

"Just what, Slade?"

"I knew something wasn't right with her, but I had no idea how wrong things were."

"Neither of us saw this coming, Slade. I came here this evening to confront Quinn. Ms. Mendez was an afterthought, after Quinn finally admitted that she was the last person to leave his home, and that she was the other woman."

"She's lost, Wintahs."

"I know, Slade. Hopefully, she can get some help. Can't say that secrets caused all of this, but they caused a lot of it."

"Yeah, that and a lot of people walking around needing help, and not getting it. She's gonna have a lot of time to work on that."

"That she will," I said as we watched Ms. Mendez being led out of the auditorium.

❧ CHAPTER 19 ❧

"Doc, you just can't make this stuff up," my secretary told me as we sat in the waiting room of my office, sipping coffee.

"I know, Kendall. Real life is so much stranger than fiction."

"I'm jus' glad that, as much of a scoundrel that he was, that Mr. Quinn survived. You know, he could be dead right now?"

"Absolutely, but he's going to be okay. He'll be sore for a while, but he's going to live."

"And what about his son, Li'l Quinn? Wonder what's gonna happen to him Doc?"

"Well, from what I understand, he's getting the best help that money can buy. But he's going to be locked up in that hospital for at least a year or so. He did break a few laws."

"Yeah, he did, but it's good to hear that he's gettin' help, 'cause he needs it, doggone it. We all need help from time to time, right, Doc?"

"You hit the nail on the head, Kendall. We all do."

"Some of us need to dial 911 on that, huh though."

"Agreed."

"Oh, and what about your publisher, Mr. Steele? I know he was fit to be tied after he got out of jail and found out what happened."

"He was, even though they only kept him overnight. I heard through the publishing grapevine that he was so shaken after that night in jail he's now on sabbatical from the publishing world."

"Well, I have it on good authority that he and Miss Ivy are separated."

"You do? I have to ask, Kendall. *What* authority?"

"*Entertainment Tonight.*" My secretary relayed that message with the straightest face. "By the way, Doc, I ran into Ms. Kane yesterday at the grocery store. And she wanted me to tell you that she was goin' back to school. She looked good, Doc."

"That is truly good news, Kendall."

"You know what Mother Franklin would say about

all this? God rest her soul."

"Tell me, Kendall. What would Mother Franklin say?"

" 'We're all in this world together, so when the ship starts sinkin' for some of us, take another look at who's really goin' down. It jus' might be you. All it takes is a helpin' hand to save a life.' "

"Well put, Mother Franklin."

*   *   *   *

"She's one of New Orleans' best kept secrets," the MC announced as I stood in the wings, listening to the introduction. I peeked from behind the curtain; once again, the auditorium was packed. I was there to deliver the speech I had almost delivered before. *How do I do this? There are no coincidences, Morgan. Can't believe that Mr. Pitre died in jail, after being picked up for being drunk and disorderly conduct. There are no coincidences,* I told myself as my stomach began to quake at the thought of speaking to the large group about this very personal thing. *What are they going to think about me? What will I think if I don't set myself free today?*

"There she is!" I heard a stage-hand say from behind. Before I could completely turn around, a massive hand on the small of my back garnered my attention.

"Where you at, there, Wintahs?" Slade whispered, and then placed a kiss on my cheek. His warm eyes and arboreal smell were a welcomed distraction.

"You, Commander Slade, are just what the doctor ordered." I turned around and gave him the gentlest of kisses on his lips as he held me in his arms. "I thought you had to work."

"I do, but first things first. A little birdie told me that you might be able to use a little extra support this morning."

"Well, that's that smartest extrasensory-perception bird ever. By the way, is it true? Are they going to shoot for a life sentence, with possible parole in thirty years for Lola Mendez?"

"That's what I'm hearing. She wants to make a deal."

"Ladies and gentlemen, the pride of New Orleans, Dr. Morgan Jane Winters!" the announcer proclaimed as the crowd cheered with anticipation.

"I'll be here when you're done. Do *you*, Wintahs. That's always more than enough." He winked one of his deep-set brown eyes as he released me from his embrace. I took comfort in his words, but more from the glimmering light reflected in his eyes.

I was welcomed with thunderous applause. I paused for a moment of reflection. *I forgive you, Mr. Pitre, and I forgive you, Morgan,* I told myself as I walked up to the podium.

"Thank you," I addressed the crowd over the ovation. "Thank you very much." They continued to cheer as I scanned the sea of faces waiting to hear me speak. The room suddenly grew quiet with the anticipation of my first words. *Dear God, let this be a blessing to someone, if not many today. I thank you,* I said in my head as I took a sip of water, followed by a deep breath, and began to speak:

"My name is Morgan Jane Winters, and I'm here today to talk to you about my guilt, my shame, and my liberating truth. That means that today's lecture is going to be full of joy, pain, forgiveness, and freedom. I'm not going to leave anything out today. I'm done hiding. Today, I'm seeking the truth. Are you ready to hear the truth?"

"Yes!" the crowd cheered as I looked off to the side and smiled at Slade, who appeared fully captivated by my presence at the rostrum. "When I was a little girl, my mother and father gave me the prettiest bike a little girl could ever want..."

Hide-and-Seek is the second installment in the groundbreaking series centered around fictional psychiatrist and part-time sleuth Dr. Morgan Jane Winters. It has been warmly dubbed "a Murder Mystery Series with a Message." *Surrender*, the first novel in the series, was met with rave reviews. If you haven't already read it, be sure to check it out. Also, you won't want to miss, **Liar**, the next book in the Morgan Jane Winters Murder Mystery Series. It's coming soon.

To know more about Jill visit her web page: www.jillcollins.net

Jill Collins was born and reared in New Orleans, LA, specifically, the historic Pontchartrain Park subdivision. She earned a Bachelor of Arts in Sociology from Tulane University and worked as a researcher at both Tulane and Louisiana State University (LSU) for over twenty years. Jill now resides in Silver Spring, MD with her husband, where she volunteers for hospice, plays her flute, and continues to write.

www.ingramcontent.com/pod-product-compliance
Lightning Source LLC
Chambersburg PA
CBHW031231120726
47905CB00002B/554